Den wondered how she would assess him. Had she done it already? He imagined the little file card; 'Den Watts: a bit flash, prone to run off at the mouth.' Did she think he was good looking? He glanced sideways at her. Could the likes of her *truly* fancy him? He skirted the thought that maybe she fancied a bit of rough, then again he wondered if it was all a take-on. He wanted confirmation.

By the same author

The Outsider
The Dark Side of the Sun

EastEnders Novels

Home Fires Burning
Swings and Roundabouts
Good Intentions
The Flower of Albert Square
Blind Spots
Hopes and Horizons
The Baffled Heart
Growing Wild
A Place in Life
A Single Man
Taking Chances
Elbow Room

HUGH MILLER

Blind Spots

EastEnders – Book 5

By arrangement with the
British Broadcasting Corporation

WITH COMPLIMENTS
OF EVER READY

GRAFTON BOOKS

A Division of the Collins Publishing Group

LONDON GLASGOW
TORONTO SYDNEY AUCKLAND

Grafton Books
A Division of the Collins Publishing Group
8 Grafton Street, London W1X 3LA

A Grafton Paperback Original 1986
Reprinted 1988 (twice)

ISBN 0-586-06813-9

Printed and bound in Great Britain by
Collins, Glasgow

Set in Times

1

On the face of it, Den didn't give much for his chances. Not if he considered his situation clearly. But right now there was something like a warm fog in his head. It got in the way of clear thinking, and it was pretty pleasant.

'Jan,' he murmured, testing the name on his lips, hearing his voice echo softly in the booth. 'Jan.'

He stared at the telephone dial, fumbling out a couple of ten-pence pieces. As his fingers hovered over the receiver he shook his head gently.

'Bloody hell, Den. What're you gettin' yourself into?'

Aiming low, that was the safe way, *his* way. Success was nearly always guaranteed, and if he occasionally failed – well, so what, he hadn't lost much, had he? This woman who was filling his mind, making him forget his own 'phone number, she was in a high target bracket, well above anything he had ever attempted before.

He positioned a coin in the slot, concentrated hard until his number came back to him, then dialled. The call tone rang out for a long time before somebody answered. Den thrust the coin into the box.

'Hello? Ange?'

'Den? Where the hell are you?' The tinny rattle of the earpiece made her voice scratchier than usual. 'You said you'd be back by four.'

'It went on a bit longer than I thought.'

'Brewery piss-ups always do.'

Den sighed. 'It wasn't a piss-up. It was a wine tastin'.'

'Yeah, well, whatever it was, it was an excuse for the lot of you to skive off an' get tanked up. When are you comin' back?'

He took a deep breath and hoped he would sound convincing. 'Somethin's come up – that's why I'm ringin' you. Mr Larkin – you know, the new Area Manager – he wants some of us to go back to Head Office with him. They're havin' a bit of a private celebration . . .'

Angie's breath struck the mouthpiece sharply. 'I hope you told him you couldn't make it.'

'What, an' risk offendin' him? Do you know what kind of trouble he could make for us if he took the hump?'

The Area Manager really had asked Den to a party, a small gathering to celebrate the expansion of the brewery's wine merchandising division. Den had refused on the grounds of work pressure. Mr Larkin hadn't been offended in the least.

'I see.' Angie's voice had gone very soft. 'I'm expected to hold the fort again, am I? Run this bleedin' pub on me todd while you get blotto with the bigwigs?'

At least she believed him, he thought. 'Ange, I'm not any happier about this than you are. But there's times when I have to be a bit diplomatic . . .'

'Cobblers.'

'I'll be back just as early as I can.' This time there was no response. 'Ange?' There was a moment's agitated breathing at the other end, then the line went

6

dead. Den put back the receiver, squared his tie and stepped out into the hotel foyer.

'All right, mate?' It was Harry Richards from the *Golden Lion*. He was one of the older and more rumpled landlords at the gathering. He grinned at Den. 'Not a bad bit of plonk, eh? Wish I could stop for more.' He gestured towards the door. 'Couldn't give us a lift back to Walford, could you? Taxi drivers don't like crossin' the river from this side.'

'Sorry,' Den said. 'The missus wants me to get a few things for her while I'm up West. I'll be an hour or so yet.' He was gazing towards the reception room where the tasting was being held. Jan was still in there somewhere, circulating. 'Maybe one of the other lads could help you out.'

Harry shrugged. 'I've got to go right now. I'm late as it is. They're all still glued in there – will be till the supplies run out, I shouldn't wonder.' He nodded a farewell and shuffled away across the foyer.

'See you, Harry.'

Den touched his tie again and moistened his lips. He couldn't remember when he had felt so dry-mouthed before. Or so jangly with anticipation: It was like being a kid again. He took a deep breath, switched on his bright, confident face and strode across to the reception room.

It took a minute to locate her. There were more than a hundred people in there, milling around the tables crammed with wine bottles and dishes of nuts and biscuits. When Den spotted her she was standing in a corner talking to two men in pinstriped suits. Some style, he thought. She was beautiful, but not in any way he could pin down. It was a combination of

7

things – the slender, smooth lines detectable under the immaculate blue suit, the way she moved, the purring, cultured sensuality of her voice. And her face. She had high, rounded cheekbones, a soft, full, mobile mouth and eyes that seemed to look past the surface, not so much penetrating as probing. And she fancied him! The fact hit him again and it was staggering.

Den turned away and found himself a drink. He would have to disappear soon, otherwise his story about being under pressure would fall through and Larkin would be at him again. He gulped back the sweetish white wine, smiled at a couple of people he knew and glanced across at Jan again. Their five-minute conversation had covered a lot of ground; he had learned a fair bit about her. She was a personnel officer with one of the big Knightsbridge stores. Her flat was a five-minute walk from her work, she liked to spend weekends golfing or playing tennis and she was very fond of the theatre. She had come to this bash with her company's wineshop manager, out of curiosity. As she talked, Den had felt a very special sensation, the same one that had trembled through him when he first laid eyes on the accountant, Ruth . . .

He thrust the comparison out of his mind. That affair had caused him a lot of trouble. It had scared him off for a few years. He had stuck to simple flirtations and the occasional quickie, until now. It had been half a flirty impulse, half genuine instinct that had made him suggest to Jan that they meet somewhere for a drink that evening. 'That would be lovely,' she said with her wonderful open smile. She suggested a place near Sloane Square. 'See you there about half-seven, shall I?' Since then Den's head had been spinning.

He sighed and swallowed some more wine. He didn't want to leave her presence, not even for a couple of short hours. There was also a small fear beginning to grow, a feeling that maybe she had just been kidding him along. Maybe she didn't intend to turn up at all.

He began edging across the room, avoiding the Area Manager, getting himself closer to Jan without making it obvious.

'Enjoyin' yourself, Den?' Jimmy Rush, a small, red-faced man who now ran Den's previous pub in Islington, was drinking alternately from a wine glass in one hand and glass of water in the other. 'I've had a drop too much, meself. I'm tryin' to dilute it a bit.'

'That's the way, Jimmy.' Den said it absently, staying on the move. 'Keep takin' the water with it. Can't go wrong.'

Three other people tried to detain him on his way across to the corner. Finally, having brushed them all off, he stopped a couple of yards from Jan and pretended to be judging the quality of his drink, rattling a mouthful around his teeth and sniffing at the rim of the glass. He could hear her talking. It was a voice that massaged the ears, he decided. Posh was hardly the word for it.

'Character assessment is a very large part of my job,' she was saying. 'I often think it's the most important part of all.'

Den wondered how she would assess him. Had she done it already? He imagined the little file card; 'Den Watts: a bit flash, prone to run off at the mouth.' Did she think he was good looking? He glanced sideways at her. Could the likes of her *truly* fancy him? He skirted the thought that maybe she fancied a bit of

9

rough, then again he wondered if it was all a take-on. He wanted confirmation.

As he turned to face her, wondering just how he would break into her conversation, Jan touched the arm of the man who was talking to her.

'Excuse me for a moment, will you?' She came forward and stepped up close to Den, bathing him in her smile. 'I thought you'd gone.'

'Just had to make a 'phone call.' He wished his voice sounded more relaxed. Women liked a man to be cool and sure of himself. 'I'm off now, though. Things to do.' He cleared his throat. 'So, I'll be seein' you a bit later, will I?'

'Half-seven, as arranged.'

He nodded. 'Right then. See you in a bit.'

As he walked away the blood began to sing in his ears. It was on! God alone knew what he was getting himself into, what layers of intrigue and coils of deceit, what downright trouble, even danger if Angie ever caught on. A straight-faced, head-shaking little man inside him said he should chuck it right now, turn his back on this before it blew up into something he couldn't handle.

'Ah, what the hell.'

Den felt himself grinning as he pushed his way out through the front doors. A man's a long time dead, he was reminding himself. He should take every bit of adventure that comes along and get the best out of it. If he didn't, he'd lie on his deathbed smothering with regret.

2

Sharon, a plump twelve-year-old on the verge of puberty, stood by the kitchen door while her mother did her best to read the riot act. Angie wasn't good at that kind of thing with Sharon. Only Den could bring out the real spitfire in her.

'There's no use denyin' it, Shar. Your teacher's letter don't make no bones. You were caught puffin' a fag in the girls' loo.'

'I'm not sayin' I didn't do it,' Sharon pouted. 'What I'm sayin' is the fag wasn't mine. They was passin' it round. I just took a puff for a laugh.'

Angie's eyes widened. 'A laugh? Have you any idea what them things can do to your lungs? Do you want to end up with a chest soundin' like an old busted squeeze-box?'

'It was only once. I hadn't done it before.'

'That's your story.'

'Does the letter say I'm a liar an' all?' Sharon snatched up her school bag. 'I'm off. I'll be late if I don't go now.'

'Listen.' Angie raised a stiff finger. 'You're goin' nowhere until you promise me this smokin' lark's over an' done with. It's a good job your dad didn't get to know about it. He'd go spare.' Sharon had held on to the letter for two days before she handed it over. 'Chances are I wouldn't have found out meself if there

11

wasn't a slip in the envelope for me to sign an' send back.'

'I just forgot to give it to you.'

'Yeah.' Angie demonstrated her disbelief with a sharp sniff. 'Well then? Do you promise?'

'Course I do.'

'It won't happen again?'

The girl shook her head, jiggling her blonde curls. 'It was only the once. Honest, Mum.'

'Right. That's that. We'll say no more about it.' The small break in Sharon's voice, calculated or not, had wiped out every trace of Angie's annoyance, which hadn't been much to begin with. She had smoked a few cigarettes herself before she was Sharon's age. She wasn't so old that she'd forgotten the excitements and temptations of school life. 'On you go, then.'

Sharon kissed her mother's cheek. 'See you at dinner time.'

As she left Angie gazed at the empty doorway for a moment, then glanced at the brewery calendar on the wall. 10th October, 1981. Her mind shifted abruptly. 10th October. That made it a week now since she had found out. She had looked at the calendar every morning since she discovered the little note on the floor beside Den's bed. She felt in the pocket of her robe and took it out again. The handwriting was firm, with bold forward-slanting strokes that denoted a lot of confidence.

Den –
I haven't run away. Make yourself a cup of coffee. I'll be back in about half an hour.

There was no signature, just one big cross. A kiss. A kiss that wounded Angie's heart every time she looked at it. She folded the pale blue paper again and put it back in her pocket, wondering why she tortured herself that way, why she counted the days since she had picked it up off the floor.

'You there, Angie?' Ethel Skinner came to the door in her overall and woolly hat. She was clutching a duster.

'No. This is a wax dummy, Ethel. I'm still in bed.'

Ethel grinned, deepening the wrinkles on her small face. 'I'm nearly out of spray polish. And I could use some Hoover bags.'

'Right, I'll see to it. Anythin' else?'

'Not that I can think of.' Ethel turned away. 'A cup of tea wouldn't go amiss, mind you.'

'Give me ten minutes.'

Angie strode out past Ethel and went into her bedroom. She shut the door and unbelted her robe. At the wardrobe she turned and looked at her bed. For nearly six years she had been sleeping there alone. She wondered again; how many married people lived like that – her in one room, him in another? She remembered no distinct reason for it coming to that. There had been no clear point in their turbulent marriage when it was decided that sex and even closeness should be ruled out. It had just become a fact with no special event behind it. A kind of evolution, Angie thought.

'The odd couple,' she mumbled, opening the wardrobe. She stared at the rows of skirts, blouses and dresses. The small mystery lingered in her. What normal married man could lose all his interest in his

13

wife, all his curiosity about her? What kind of bloke could keep his hands off his missus for years on end, yet still go through all the other public and private rituals of marriage? Her lips tightened as another thought occurred; what type of woman could keep her mouth shut and her hands off her old man's throat when she found out he'd been seeing another woman?

She shook herself and unhooked a skirt from the rail. Life went on. Routine and duty pushed everything into perspective. As she ran her finger along the row of blouses she forced herself to hum the latest Number One.

Den came up from the cellar to find Detective Sergeant Grazier leaning on the bar. The policeman's presence was never good news. Den put on a grin.

'We're not open yet, squire.'

'I know that.'

'Still, if it's really urgent, I can let you have one on the house.' Den came across and leaned opposite Grazier. 'What'll it be?'

'An explanation, Mr Watts. That'd suit me just fine.'

Den made his grin turn to puzzlement. He was close enough to smell Grazier's terrible aftershave and the onion-tinged odour of his breath. Without the job he did, the big detective would be a regular candidate for Slob of the Month. His oily hair, small ferrety eyes, cheese-slab face and cut-price clothes gave him the look of a third-rate bookie's runner. But he was the Law, so appearances counted for nothing. He was staring at Den now the way a tomcat would gaze at a lame starling.

'I don't follow, Mr Grazier.'

The detective reached in his pocket and took out a twenty packet of Silk Cut. He held it in front of Den's eyes.

'Recognize these?'

Den nodded. 'They're fags. We sell them all the time.'

Grazier sighed. 'Don't tit around, eh? These were purchased in here last night. They didn't come from the machine, they were out of a carton on the back shelf.' He lowered the packet as his other hand came up, one finger pointing. 'That carton, if I'm not mistaken.'

Den glanced at the half-empty box and shrugged. 'So what?'

'So the alert off-duty constable who bought these cigarettes detected an irregularity and brought them straight to me.' The packet came up before Den's eyes again, side-on this time. 'Notice anything strange, Mr Watts?'

Den squinted at the packet. 'Can't say I do.'

'There's something missing.' Grazier eased himself to his full height. He pushed the packet a fraction closer to Den. 'No government health warning.'

Den's eyes wavered. 'Bit of a cock-up at the printer's, d'you reckon?'

'No cock-up,' Grazier said sternly. 'These are duty-free cigarettes, Mr Watts. It's an offence for you to sell them.'

'What?' Innocence and outrage chased each other across Den's face. 'I don't get it. I mean, I bought them fags in good faith . . .'

'Where?'

Again Den's eyes flickered. 'Well, it could have

been one or two places – I mean I use a lot of wholesale outlets, one way an' another . . .'

Grazier's lips twisted sourly. 'You're saying you don't know where they came from?'

'Not for sure. I often nip out an' buy a couple of hundred when the machine runs out of a particular brand. I got that lot maybe two, three days ago.'

Angie came downstairs at that point. She was in a tight blue skirt, ruffed white blouse and shiny black high-heeled shoes. Her glossed lips opened in a wide smile when she saw the detective.

'Well, well. How long's it been since we last saw you, Mr Grazier?'

The change in the Inspector was remarkable. Like all men who are unattractive to women, he believed he had a hidden, magnificent charm that only certain females could detect and respond to. Angie Watts, he was sure, was one such woman. He returned her smile, putting as much warmth into it as he could.

'It's been a couple of months, I suppose. Nice to see you again, Mrs Watts.'

'Don't be so formal,' Angie chided. She ignored Den's glare as she moved up kittenishly to the bar. 'The name's Angie, an' well you know it.' She leaned forward, wafting her perfume across the policeman. 'I hope this is a social call.'

Grazier tried for a look of deep regret. 'Fraid not,' he said, flicking his eyes towards Den, inviting him to explain.

'Looks like somebody turned us over with a carton of dodgy fags,' Den muttered.

'Duty-frees, Mrs Watts – ah, Angie, I mean.'

'God no, really?'

Grazier nodded. 'You'll appreciate the matter has to be looked into . . .'

'Well of course it has.' Angie looked at Den. 'Where'd they come from?' she asked him sharply.

'Can't remember, just at the moment.'

'God, Den, you've got a memory like a sieve.'

Grazier watched Den shuffle his feet. He'd never had any doubt that the landlord of *The Queen Victoria* was a villain. He was perfectly convinced the cigarettes had been acquired in a shady deal, a deal in which Den Watts had come off badly, simply because he didn't have the same amount of savvy as the crooks he dealt with. Grazier had long wanted a chance to nail Den and he was sure this was it.

Then he looked at Angie. There was definitely a lot of promise there; Grazier had thought it before and now, seeing the way she returned his glance, sensing the heat beneath the friendly calm, he was sure of it. If he played it cool enough there was a definite opportunity for some hanky-panky. Lately, the Inspector had been very short of hanky-panky. Weighing his feelings about both people, he decided he would do himself a favour by doing one for Den. He could always nab him another time.

'Look, Mr Watts . . .' Grazier spread his hands in an open gesture. 'I've no doubt you were the victim of a swindle here.' He saw Den's cautious frown but carried on smoothly. 'Somebody somewhere unloaded a stack of duty-frees on you and you didn't notice. If you should ever remember who it was, let us know and we'll do the rest. End of story, as far as I'm concerned.' The relief and gratitude on Angie's face definitely enhanced his standing with her, he reckoned. 'I'll make out a report to that effect. OK?'

'Well . . .' Den blinked at him. 'It's very decent of you, Inspector.'

'Not at all. It's not my job to victimize people, after all. Especially not when they've been victimized already.'

Angie grinned and reached forward to pat Grazier's hand. 'You're a good sort, Mr Grazier.' She made the shadow of a wink. 'It must be a right chore, havin' to deal with gullible dopes like my old man all the time.'

Grazier, thrilled by the contact of Angie's hand, smiled and nodded at the carton on the back shelf. 'I'll leave you with what's left, Mr Watts, since it's no offence to possess them. Just be sure they don't accidentally go on sale.'

'They won't,' Den grunted.

'I'll see to it,' Angie said with another little wink. 'He's like a kid. Needs supervisin' all the time.' As Den glared at her she leaned close to Grazier again. 'How about a little drinkie, while you're here?'

'I'd love to, Angie, but . . .' Grazier looked at his watch and began edging towards the door. 'A policeman's lot, and all that. I'm well behind already.' He tried to give her a special look of his own, something Den couldn't decipher. 'I might drop by one evening, though, and take you up on the offer.'

'You do that. An' make it soon.' To the Inspector's great pleasure Angie winked at him one more time before he left.

As the door swung shut Den banged the side of his fist on the bar. 'That bloody Tim Duffy! I'll knock his soddin' teeth through the back of his head!'

Angie propped her elbow on the bar and stared at him. 'What're you on about?'

'Duffy flogged me them fags.'

'You must have known they were bent.'

'Yeah, but I didn't know it showed on the packets.'

Angie tilted her head and said sweetly, 'You should pay more attention to what you're buyin', my love.' Her face hardened suddenly. 'The way you've been behavin' lately, he could have sold you a box of dog-ends an' you wouldn't have noticed.'

'Leave it out, Ange . . .'

'It's true. You walk about here with half your mind on the job an' the other half God-knows-where. Don't think I haven't noticed. Don't think most of the punters haven't, neither.' For an instant she was tempted to confront him with what she knew, the big secret she believed was behind all his vagueness and absent-mindedness. She swallowed the impulse. More proof was needed before she did anything like that. 'You want to pull yourself together an' that's a fact.'

'There's nothin' up with me.' Den lifted the carton of cigarettes and hurled it through the doorway to the back. 'There'll be somethin' up with Tim Duffy when I get hold of him, mind you.'

'Drop it. You've probably done him as many times as he's done you. Besides, it's all fixed now. No sweat. Your little Angie used her charm on the naughty big policeman.'

'Didn't you just.' Den stepped back, eyeing her up and down. 'Anythin' in trousers an' you're at it, aren't you?'

The remark stung her, but Angie smiled sweetly again. 'I just keep my femininity tickin' over, love, in case somebody finds a use for it.' Before Den could come back at her she moved smartly through to the rear and got her coat. 'I've shoppin' to do,' she told Den airily, slipping on the coat and belting it. 'I'll be back before openin' time, in case you start forgettin' the prices of things.'

When she had gone Den got a glass and pushed it up under the brandy optic. After the first amber measure had trickled into the glass he pushed again, drawing another. He held the double under his nose for a second, then drank it in three gulps. The immediate effect wasn't exactly soothing, but it distracted him for a moment. By the time his breathing settled, the warmth had begun to spread in his stomach.

'Bloody women,' he growled.

He went through to the rear and snatched up the telephone, then banged it down again. What was the use? Jan wouldn't be back for another twenty-four hours, maybe longer. She'd been gone for three days and he knew there wasn't any chance of her being back early. She had told him so.

'Damn, damn . . .'

Those three days had seemed endless. Even though he rarely saw her more than once a week, it was always a comfort to know she was only a few minutes' drive away. Except now she wasn't. She was in Zurich at a conference. The thought of her being at such a distance from him had had a devastating effect on Den. He couldn't sleep, he had scarcely eaten and he couldn't keep his mind on anything. The dragon had noticed and so had a lot of other people, just like she said. He was like a lovesick teenager, not a mature man who'd been having a mature affair for the best part of a year.

He went back to the bar and thought about pouring himself another drink. He decided against it. He'd stay sober and face his misery like a man. It was all so crazy, he thought. Being in love was supposed to be something happy, something light-headed and bulging with joy. Instead of that he was obsessed with dark thoughts about Jan, wondering where she was and what she was doing. She could be doing anything over there in Switzerland, mixing it with all the business nobs and getting chatted up by a lot of smooth talkers with as much style as they had cash.

He had just decided to distract himself by setting out the beer mats on the tables when the door eased open and Pauline Fowler put her head around the edge.

'Den, you got a minute?'

'For you my love, an hour if need be.' He made a tight smile at her. 'What's on your mind?'

Pauline came in, digging in her coat pocket. 'It's these . . .' She brought out a packet of Silk Cut. 'I got them off you yesterday. There's nothin' wrong with them, except Arthur noticed – '

'Yeah, he would,' Den snapped. He took a pile of change from his pocket and picked through it. 'Hold out your hand, Pauline.' He counted the price of twenty cigarettes on to her palm. 'Full refund, madam. It was a mistake. Bit of a foul-up on the purchasin' front, know what I mean? Keep the fags.'

'Oh . . .' Pauline looked puzzled. 'Well, that's very nice of you . . .'

'I'm that kind of bloke.'

Pauline had turned a little pink. 'I feel awful about it now. I mean, I didn't really come in to complain . . .'

'Nobody ever does, Pauline. That's why I've got such a sunny disposition. In here it's sweetness an' light, mornin' to night.'

Pauline frowned at him. 'You feelin' all right?'

'Never better. Now if you'll excuse me, I've got to get this place in shape for the forthcomin' revels.'

Pauline retreated to the door, pocketing the money and the cigarettes. 'Be seein' you, then,' she mumbled awkwardly.

'Bye.'

As she went out Den dropped the stack of beer mats and went to the telephone again. He'd thought of a much better way to distract himself and work off some of the frustration while he was at it. He'd call up Tim Duffy and lay a few extravagant threats on him.

He picked up the receiver and paused, picturing the loathsome Inspector Grazier, all poised to put the boot in, before Angie diverted him with her usual tactics. He thought of Angie herself, forever taking opportunities to make him look like a wally, in public *and* in private. He thought of that collective aggro piled on to his present misery over Jan. That was more than enough to put some steam behind his message to Mr Duffy, he decided, and began to dial.

'All that piggin' hassle,' he grunted, 'plus them other nine cartons of duty-frees stacked in me wardrobe.'

3

On the morning she looked at the kitchen calendar and realized she had known Den's secret for a whole month, Angie made a decision. A notion that had been forming in her head for over two weeks was now suddenly a plan; by resolving to follow it through, Angie started to feel a lot better. She didn't have to force herself to hum a tune that morning, and by the time she was dressed she had actually begun to whistle.

At eleven o'clock, while Den was out collecting some cases of Scotch and vodka from an Asian contact, Kathy Beale came into the bar. She had been doing a half-hour stint on her husband Pete's fruit and vegetable stall and in her own estimation she was frozen to the bone.

'I'll have a small port, Angie.' She got on to a bar stool and sat rubbing her hands vigorously. 'On second thoughts, make it a big one.'

'It's not like you to start boozin' at this time of day,' Angie observed. She uncorked the port bottle and grinned. 'Somethin' to do with your age, I expect. I've noticed the old dears round here start tipplin' in the mornin's as soon as their glands begin witherin'.'

'Cheeky cow.' They were best friends, and one feature of the friendship was that they could fire insults back and forward without causing each other the slightest offence. 'If my glands have started to wither, God knows what state yours are in, Grannie.'

'As it happens,' Angie said, lowering her voice, 'my old glandular set-up is feelin' pretty good this mornin'.'

Kathy peered at her carefully as she handed over the drink. 'You do look a bit chirpy, now you mention it. In fact, I'd say I haven't seen you look this bright in a long time.' She sipped her drink, still watching Angie. 'What're you up to?'

'Improvin' me lot.'

'What's that mean?'

'I'm takin' a new direction. Changin' me outlook. Doin' somethin' about givin' life a bit more meanin'.'

Kathy sighed. 'That means you've either got religion, or you've fixed your sights on another man.'

Angie mimed shock. 'Kath! How could you say such a thing?'

'Because I know you. Come on, stop beatin' about the bush. What's goin' on?'

'It's only at the plannin' stage yet. Maybe I'll let you know later. But I'll tell you this much for now.' Angie folded her arms and leaned her elbows on the bar. 'You know what happens when somebody drops a burnin' fag end on the carpet – it smoulders away, burnin' an' burnin' at the fabric until somebody steps on it.'

'Eh?' Kathy was staring at her, her mouth half open.

'I'm steppin' on the fag that's been burnin' me own fabric. That's what I'm up to.'

Kathy nodded slowly, like someone humouring a child. 'You sure you haven't been at the bottle yourself?'

Angie giggled as she turned away to serve another customer. Kathy watched her, noting the bouncy way she moved, the brisk cheerfulness of her. There had been a time, a year ago, when Angie behaved like that for nearly a month. She was always naturally cheerful and bouncy behind the bar but her behaviour then, as now, was different, it had an added edge of brightness and energy. At the end of that month in 1980 Angie had suddenly taken a dive. She moped and wept and got drunk nearly every night for a week. The reason behind both the brightness and the sudden depression had been a man. Kathy suspected she could see history on the verge of repeating itself. When Angie came back along the bar she tackled her directly.

'You're not settin' up a load of heartbreak for yourself again, are you?'

Angie's smile remained, but it became rather fixed. 'What're you on about?'

'Men, that's what. You were just like this the last time. Bright as a button, full of bounce, then he dropped you an' wallop! you went doomy an' gloomy, got legless all the time an' kept goin' on about life havin' no meanin' – '

'Listen,' Angie interrupted sharply. Her smile had gone. 'You might be my best mate, Kath, but there's a limit to how far you can shove your nose an' your opinions.'

'I'm not bein' nosey, I'm just warnin' you. Havin' an affair is just a way to buy misery. Why go hurtin' yourself? It's a mug's game.'

Angie glared. 'So you're an expert, are you?'

'I've got eyes in me head.'

Angie took a slow, deep breath. Her features soft-ened. 'Let's not go all unfriendly, Kath. You're the last person I want to have a row with.'

'I don't want one either. I was only tryin' to remind

you. Messin' about with other men might seem rosy and excitin' at the beginnin', but it soon turns rotten.'

'Not for some people.'

'But for you it does.' Kathy took a swig from her glass. 'It *is* a man, isn't it? Nothin' else gets you goin' all sparkly.'

Angie shrugged. 'Nothin's settled yet. Like I said, it's at the plannin' stage.'

'But what for?' Kathy demanded. 'Why not spend your energy improvin' things between you an' Den?'

'It's because of Den I'm makin' me plans.'

Kathy frowned. 'What do you mean?'

'I mean he's got somebody else.'

'Aw, come on . . .'

'What's so unlikely about it?' Angie's mouth tightened suddenly. Her eyes went distant for a moment, as if she were scanning the hurt inside herself. 'He's done it before, after all.'

'So have you,' Kathy said quietly.

'The reasons were different. Den had everything on offer at home. I'd nothin'. He wouldn't even set foot in my bedroom, let alone climb in the bed . . .'

Kathy began to look embarrassed. 'Angie, don't tell me. I'm sorry I brought this up, it's your business after all – '

'Have you any idea what it's like, livin' with a man who doesn't want to know?' Angie was talking in a strained whisper. It hit the air like a growl. 'I'm thirty-four years old. Since I was twenty-eight my so-called husband hasn't laid a lovin' finger on me. Can you imagine that? *Can* you? What if your Pete was the same way with you? How would you feel?'

'I'd leave him.'

26

Angie swallowed hard and stared at the bartop. 'Yeah, I suppose you would.'

'But instead of leavin' Den, you hang on an' try scorin' points off him. You're not even doin' it because you fancy somebody else. You're out for revenge.' Kathy stopped abruptly and emptied her glass. 'Look, I'll say it again, I'm sorry. A mate should know the limits. I'll not poke me nose in again.' She got off the stool. 'Just be careful, Angie, eh?'

'Yeah.' Angie turned away. Behind her she heard Kathy leave. The bright mood had evaporated, she realized. What she felt now was just a hollow, not even sadness. That was a pity; if she hadn't been obliged to face the facts for a moment, she could have gone on feeling good. The truth had a way of always making Angie feel empty or sad or angry. But never very happy. That said a lot about the kind of truths that made up her life.

Somebody tapped the bar and she turned. Her heart jolted. She couldn't believe it for a moment. There he was, standing right there at the bar. Her target. Angie brightened at once.

'It's that time again,' Jimmy Solomon said, dangling a thick bunch of keys. He had come to empty the fruit machine.

Angie beamed at him. 'A fortnight whips round fast, don't it?'

'Yeah. I'm a day early, mind you.'

She was radiant again. It wasn't just on the surface, she was sparkling right through. Cold facts had fled; this was show time, game time. 'Fancy a drink before you get down to it?'

'Wouldn't say no. A half of Churchill, please.'

As she pulled the drink Angie told herself this was an omen. Nothing could be clearer. That very morning she had decided to make a play for Jimmy Solomon. Lo and behold, in he walks not three hours later, hot on the heels of Kath's little pep talk – *and he was one day early*! If that wasn't a go-ahead from her stars, she didn't know what was.

'There you go.' She put the glass in front of Jimmy. 'On the house.' She gave him her best, warmest smile.

'Cheers,' he murmured.

For the next five minutes, as she served customers up and down the bar, Angie kept stealing glances at Jimmy. He was younger than she was, maybe thirty, a tall, well-built man with dark wavy hair and sensual, slightly heavy features. He had a lot of physical grace, she had noticed; when he moved it was as if the actions had been planned and rehearsed to perfection, with not a single excessive movement in his step or gesture. He even made the act of beer-drinking look elegant.

Angie came forward as he emptied his glass. 'Another one?' she asked.

'No, I'd better get on with the job.' His smile, full-lipped and generous, narrowed his eyes and put up Angie's pulse-rate. 'Thanks all the same.'

He got to work on the bandit as Angie began working on her approach. Earlier, she had decided to spend the first part of the day simply anticipating her little adventure, then she thought she would devise her tactics in the afternoon and evening. Jimmy's appearance on the scene had short-circuited all that. As she pulled beer and tried to decide on her opening ploy, another short-circuit occurred. Den came back a full two hours earlier than he had said he would.

Angie stared at him as he stacked boxes at the foot of the stairs. 'I thought you said you'd be having a bit of lunch with Ali Whatsisname?'

'He was too busy.' Den stepped back from the pile of boxes and made a humourless smile at her. 'I'll just have to dine with you instead, my precious.' He straightened his tie and pushed past her into the bar. 'Oh God,' he groaned.

'What's up?'

'Soppy Solomon's here again. He gives me the creeps, that bloke.'

'Makes you feel insecure, does he?' Angie murmured.

'What's he got that'd make me feel insecure?'

'Well, he's got looks. A build. Style.'

Den's eyes widened. 'Style? He walks like a poof.'

Sudden, defensive anger gripped Angie. It wasn't bad enough that he'd got back early and complicated things – he had to start slandering the very man she was after. 'You're eaten up with jealousy every time you see a young, good-lookin' male in this pub, aren't you? Beats me why you don't ban any bloke that's under sixty or hasn't got a hump and warts.'

Den stamped across to serve a customer. As he turned to put the money in the till he flashed his teeth at Angie. 'So you fancy old oily-chops, do you?'

Now she felt caution. She had overshot. Den was good at deducing things from her behaviour. 'Don't be so bloody daft,' she hissed.

'Oh, it wouldn't surprise me, Ange.' Den's tone was light and poisonously amiable. 'You've been showin' a bit of an interest in creeps. A lot more interest as time passes, I've noticed. Somethin' to do with the change, maybe.' He winked. 'Can't be far off now, can it?'

'Who needs the opinions of a man that can't even do his simple marital duties?'

He didn't blink. 'There's duty an' there's punishment, Ange. Don't get them confused.' He lowered his voice; 'I can always rise to the occasion if I'm given somethin' vaguely resemblin' temptation.'

Angie didn't want this. He was unsettling her, humiliating her. She could never go through with her plans in this state, even if she got a chance. 'Why don't you just shut your face an' get on with seein' to the punters?' she said lamely.

'Right away, darlin'.' He pointed towards the corner, where Jimmy was emptying out the bandit's coin box. 'An' while I'm doin' that, why don't you have a little break? Go over there an' sweeten up the fruit-machine man.' He smiled again. 'You never know your luck. He might fancy old birds as much as they seem to fancy him.'

She could have hit him. Instead, she marched smartly through to the back and ran up the stairs. In the kitchen she sat down and clasped her hands tightly on the table.

'That *bastard!*'

She was shaking. Tears were stinging her eyes. Frustration, hurt and something terribly like hatred were filling her head and tightening her throat. It would have been easy for her to believe he had been sent to her as a curse. All her misery was down to Den, every deep unhappiness she harboured could be traced right back to him, and when she tried to even the balance, what happened? Den stepped in sharply to thwart her and add a bit of extra pain for good measure. At that moment, as she swallowed back a sob and tried to stop herself trembling, she wished death on Den Watts. It would only be justice, she reasoned. He had deprived her of affection and pride, he had diminished her life and dwarfed every hope of things ever improving. He was her curse and always would be as long as he breathed.

After a few minutes she began to feel less agitated. Hatred for Den shrank to simple loathing. She unclenched her hands and flattened them on her knees. Somewhere deep down in her, defiance was glowing. It always did, in the end. Defiance kept her going. Defiance and revenge.

'You wait an' see,' she whispered, picturing Den's sneering face. She would go after Jimmy Solomon, no matter what. She would learn to ignore the jibes and the sarcasm that always made her blow her cool. She would get back at her heartless, womanizing swine of a husband and taunt him with it. 'Wait an' see, Denny boy . . .'

Down in the bar Den was talking to Ali Osman, a Cypriot mini-cab driver who shared Den's interest in games of chance, particularly poker. Ali had brought news of a game that was being set up for the following Saturday. Den was being reluctantly tempted.

'I don't know about these all-night games, Ali. I get right knackered, then I've got to open up the pub an' work all day. Besides, I lost eighty quid the last one of them I went to with you.'

'This is your chance to make it back,' Ali told him. 'Right bunch of mugs, Den. Beginners, with plenty to throw about. Just the kind of set-up you like.'

'I enjoy a *bit* of a challenge,' Den protested.

'You'll get that, too. I'll be playin', remember.'

Den sniffed. 'I'll have to think about it, mate. Have to square it with the wife, an' all.'

'I've told mine I'll be on the cabbyin' all night. Swallowed it in one, she did.'

'You've got the advantage on me there.' Den shrugged. 'My old woman's behavin' a bit odd, just lately. Keeps givin' me funny looks. An' I get enough verbals off her as it is, without puttin' her back up over some poker game.' He thought for a moment. 'Tell you what. Drop in some time this evenin' if you can, I'll let you know then.'

'Right.' Ali downed the dregs of his lager and moved away from the bar. 'Do your best, won't you? We could both make a killin' on this one.'

As Ali went out Jimmy Solomon brought the tally sheet to the bar to be signed. He asked Den how business was doing.

'Can't complain,' Den muttered, making his squiggle on the paper.

'It's a popular place, The Vic. Your missus has a lot to do with that, I reckon.'

Den dropped the pen and stared at him. 'How d'you mean?'

Jimmy caught the hostile light in Den's eye. 'Well, she's bright an' cheery an' all that,' he said cautiously. 'Always makes the customers feel welcome.'

'Some more than others, maybe.' Den's voice had gone terribly cold. He was still staring. Jimmy stared back, a little helplessly. 'Was there anythin' else?' Den enquired.

'No, no, that's it, chief.' Glad to be off the hook,

Jimmy put the sheet in his bag and snapped it shut. 'See you next time round, then.'

'Yeah.'

Den watched him go, still feeling that odd sensation, the one he always got when a young man passed a compliment about Angie. He could swear it was jealousy. But how the hell, he wondered, could he possibly be jealous? It was Jan he loved, not Angie.

4

'Human bein's are a funny lot,' Ethel said. Her little pug dog, Willie, snuffled briefly at her ear and rested his head on her shoulder.

Lou Beale nodded and cast a dark glance along the bar. 'Some's a lot funnier than others.'

The focus of their attention was Reg Cox, a man whose natural lack of charm had widened over the years, rendering him almost an outcast. Reg liked nobody in the district and there wasn't a soul in Albert Square, so far as Lou and Ethel knew, who could abide him. Yet Reg stayed on in the Square, occupying a single room at Number 23 and spending most evenings alone in a corner seat at The Vic.

'If he don't stop pickin' his nose soon, I'll throw up me dinner,' Lou said.

'Don't watch,' Ethel advised her. 'Just ignore the dirty old devil.'

Lou glanced about her, seeking distraction. There were evenings when it simply wasn't enough to sit there with a glass of Guinness and natter to Ethel. Tonight Lou needed extra diversion. She'd had a hard day, what with helping her daughter Pauline with the washing, settling dinner-time and teatime arguments between her grandchildren Michelle and Mark, doing the shopping and coping with the multiple strains of living under the same roof as four people who regarded her, in the main, as a cantankerous, interfering old bag.

'What's he doin' here again?' she demanded suddenly.

Ethel peered. 'Who?'

'Him fiddlin' with the fruit machine. He emptied it only the other night. I saw him.'

Angie's ears were tuned by experience to pick up any conversation she wanted to. She came to the corner of the bar and leaned across to Lou. 'It's got somethin' wrong with it,' she said briskly. 'Won't pay out. The chap's come to give it the once-over.'

Lou appeared satisfied. She let her eyes roam elsewhere. Angie went further along the bar, served a customer with a pint, then moved on to the far end, where Jimmy Solomon was staring at the bandit and absently scratching his neck.

'Found the trouble, have you?'

Jimmy turned. 'As far as I can tell, it's OK. I mean I played the two quid you gave me an' it's behaved normal.' He held out his hand. It was full of coins and tokens. 'You've made a profit, actually. But like I said when you called, I'm not really the man to check it. I've picked up a thing or two about these beasts, but the service engineer's the bloke to check it out properly.'

Angie took the money and dropped it on the back shelf. 'Well,' she said, 'we'll see how it goes from now on. If it starts actin' up again, I'll get on to the service man.' She smiled brightly and spread her hands on the bar. 'How about a drink for your trouble?'

Jimmy said he'd have a whisky, since he was off duty. As Angie put the glass to the optic she felt a small tingle of anticipation. She had got him here, which was the first phase, and now she would glide into phase two, the chat-up. The hardest part was over, as far as she was concerned. It had taken her a while to get hold of Jimmy's personal 'phone number, and then she'd had to cook up a plausible reason for getting him into the bar. From here on it was a doddle.

'Your husband havin' a night off, is he?' Jimmy asked as she passed the drink to him.

'Yeah. Well sort of. He's got a bit of business somewhere.' Business, she thought wryly. It was duvet covers and fitted sheets this time; last time, the excuse had been a bargain batch of blank cassette tapes. She knew the kind of business he was up to and she didn't care. It gave her the chance to get down to some business of her own.

'What about your other half, Jimmy?' she knew he wasn't married, but it would be nice to know just what kind of opposition there was.

'Oh, I live on me own,' he said. 'I've got used to it.'

'What? You've not even got a girlfriend?'

Jimmy shook his head. 'Not at present.'

'That's surprisin' – I mean, a good-lookin' fella like you, I'd have thought somebody would have snapped you up by now.'

'I'm a careful operator, Mrs Watts . . .'

'It's Angie.' She winked. 'I like a man who's careful.' She put her elbows on the bar and treated him to the wide-eyed stare. 'Seriously though, don't you get a bit lonely without a bit of female campanionship?'

'Sometimes.' Jimmy swirled his drink thoughtfully. 'There's compensations to bein' on your own, though.'

'Such as?'

36

He shrugged. 'Lots of things. I like food, for instance. I mean real food, in good restaurants. When I fancy a meal I can go where I please, I don't have to take somebody else's tastes into consideration.'

Angie frowned carefully, trying to make no more wrinkles than she could help. 'But there's bound to be young women that share your tastes . . .'

'Most girls I've been out with – well, they've not been into food. They mostly reckoned Chinese grub or a bit of Indian was somethin' really special. I'd never have got them past the doors of an Italian restaurant.'

Angie was alert to any hand-hold she could find. Here was a big one. 'Italian? You like Italian food?'

'I love it.'

'Lord, that's a coincidence. I just adore goin' to Italian places.'

Jimmy looked impressed. 'What's your favourite meal?'

The panic light went on in Angie's head. She struggled to remember what she'd had the last time she ate Italian food. It had been years ago. 'Well, you know the way they do veal . . .'

'Oh yes,' Jimmy grinned. 'Nobody does it better. *A la Valdostana*, eh? An' have you tried Brozheloni?'

'Yeah.' Angie smiled uncertainly. 'I just like all of it. The style of cookin', the atmosphere in them places . . .' She let her smile die. 'Pity of it is, I never get the experience nowadays. My old man's more into fish an' chips. He don't like restaurants.'

'That's a shame. He doesn't know what he's missin'.'

At that very moment Angie was sure the opening would come. It only needed one more nudge from her and he would have to ask her out. There were ways of doing that kind of thing, ways to overcome the fact that she was married and not officially available for dinner dates. She was an expert at clearing the small social hurdles, but an expert needed elbow room. The arrival of Detective Inspector Grazier cramped her suddenly. He stepped up to the bar and nodded.

'Evenin', Angie.'

She tried not to scowl at him. 'Hello, Inspector. Nice to see you again.' She noticed that the mention of his rank made Jimmy look instantly uneasy. 'What'll it be?'

'I just thought I'd take you up on your invitation.'

Angie looked blank. 'What invitation?'

'To pop in and have a drink.'

'Oh, yes, of course.' She threw an apologetic glance at Jimmy, who was draining his glass. 'What'll it be, then?'

'Vodka, thanks. With a drop of lime.' As Angie went to the optic Grazier slid a stool into place and sat down. He looked coldly at Jimmy for a moment, as if he had no right to be there.

'Right then, Angie . . .' Jimmy put down his empty glass and moved away from the bar. 'Nice seein' you again. Remember, if there's any more trouble with the machine . . .'

'Hang on.' Angie slapped down Grazier's drink and picked up Jimmy's glass. 'No need to rush away. Have another one.'

'No thanks.' Jimmy went to the door. 'I promised myself an early night. See you again soon.'

'Yeah, right.' Angie made a little wave of farewell. Her smile could barely hold up.

'Friend of yours?' Grazier asked in a policeman's tone.

'An acquaintance.' She stared at Grazier, taking in his characterless features and his greasy hair. If there was anyone in the world she less wanted to see, she couldn't think who. 'Off duty, are you?'

'I'm afraid not.' Grazier pointed at the drink. 'Let me pay you for this . . .' He made no effort to reach for money.

'No, no, it's on us.'

'Well it's kind of you, in the circumstances.'

Angie cocked her head. 'How d'you mean?'

'There's been a bit of a development over that business with the cigarettes.' Grazier cleared his throat. 'At first I imagined it was just a random batch of legitimate duty-frees your husband had bought – you know, somebody's allocation, flogged for a bit of profit. But that doesn't appear to be the case.' He sipped his drink briefly. 'Is he around at all, your husband?'

Angie shook her head. 'He's out. Don't know when he'll be back.'

'Ah, well.' Grazier sighed. 'I'll hang on for a bit, in case he shows up. I'll need to talk to him soon.'

'Is it anythin' serious?'

'Could be,' Grazier murmured. 'We'll see.'

Lou Beale was waving her glass at the other end of the bar. Angie went along to serve her.

'He's a copper, isn't he?' Lou whispered hoarsely.

'That's right.' Angie jerked the top off a bottle of Guinness and poured it.

'Is he here on business?'

'Just a social call,' Angie said. She put down the

glass and picked up Ethel Skinner's. 'I think he fancies me.'

Lou giggled as Angie opened another bottle and began to pour. What did she have to do, she wondered, to set up a bit of the extra-maritals without getting snookered at every turn? The thought was pushed aside by another; what had her dummy of a husband dropped them in this time?

'There you go, girls.' Angie glanced along the bar as Lou and Ethel took their drinks. Grazier was smiling at her. She smiled back, wishing quite fervently that the floor would open and swallow him.

'The expense of spirit in a waste of shame,' Jan said, 'is lust in action.'

Den pulled the duvet further up over his stomach and made a sucking noise through his teeth. 'Is that poetry again?' he asked.

Jan turned from the little expresso machine, sitting on its own table near the bedroom door. 'Yes. The very best poetry.'

'Who this time? Betjeman? Eliot?'

'No.' Jan brought the steaming cups to the bedside table and put them down. 'Do you want a brandy?'

Den thought about it. 'Yeah, I think I do.'

She took a bottle of Remy Martin from the cabinet. 'Big one?'

'A single will do fine.'

Den rolled on his side, watching her. Jan's nakedness, as he had noticed so many times before, was more like a superb kind of clothing. At 29 her body was slender and supple, without a blemish. His gaze strayed from the sheen of her hips to the fine tapering thighs that scarcely touched where they met her body. As she bent over the glasses her breasts remained firm, without a hint of slackness. Several times Den had struggled with the notion that her body and mind somehow matched; they both had a remarkable compactness and grace.

'So tell me,' Den said as she passed him his glass.

'What?'

'Who wrote it?'

'Guess.'

'I don't know much about poetry. In fact I know bugger-all about it, except what you've told me.' He had been encouraged to read some snatches from *Summoned by Bells*, and one night Jan had recited part of Eliot's *The Waste Land*.

'It's definitely somebody you've heard of,' Jan said encouragingly.

'It sounds a bit modern.' He sipped some brandy and swished it gently around his mouth before he swallowed. 'Say it again, will you?'

Jan repeated the lines.

'You're sure it's somebody I've heard of?'

'Yes.'

Den concentrated. In the space of a year he had learned a lot of things from her. He could now face the fact that literature, poetry and art in general were not only everyone's property, they were available to anyone who pursued them with a bit of enthusiasm. He had sat entranced as Jan read to him from D. H. Lawrence, Shaw, Joyce and Yeats. He had got rid of a lot of wooden-headed prejudices and discovered he *liked* fine language and sharp observation.

'Do you give up?' Jan asked softly, sitting on the edge of the bed.

'Give me another minute.'

The thing that puzzled Den, deeply, was how the likes of Jan could love the likes of him. The thought occurred to him again as he wondered about those two lines of verse; what did he do for her? Why did she adore him, as she said she did and regularly proved she did?

'I'm stumped,' he confessed at last.

Jan smiled at him. 'It was Shakespeare,' she said.

'Really? Christ, it sounds a lot later than him.'

'He was always ahead of his time.' Jan drew up her knees and slid closer to him. 'Those are the opening lines of the one-hundred and twenty-ninth sonnet. You should go through the sonnets some time.'

'Yeah. I can just see meself, quotin' a couple of them before closin' time every Saturday.' He reached for his coffee cup and took a gulp. As he set the cup down again he sighed. 'I'll have to be goin', love.'

'I know.'

'I don't want to, but . . .'

'But a person with two lives has to stick to the rules. It hurts, but it makes sense.' Jan ruffled his hair. 'Have you any idea how much I love you? I've tried to tell you.'

'I know you have. And I've listened.'

She leaned closer still and kissed him. 'Do you think you love me as much?'

'It's likely.' Den stared at her. Every meeting was a renewal of the miracle. This beautiful woman, with her possessions, status, classy escorts and impeccable pedigree, loved no one but him. He still couldn't believe it, even though he didn't doubt it, either.

'How long do you think we can go on like this, Jan?'

She didn't hesitate. 'As long as we both want,' she said.

He shook his head. 'There's times I wonder at it. You and me. It's a bit miraculous, in its way.'

'Nonsense. I see it as inevitable.' Her voice had a ring of authority that sometimes carried an imperious note. Now, she realized she had spoken like a school teacher and she immediately looked apologetic. 'Sorry, Den. The dogmatic approach gets to be a habit in my line of work. I didn't mean to contradict you.' She touched his arm. 'What I mean is, I knew there was someone in the world, someone like you, that I would meet and want to be with for good.'

'You really reckon it's for good?'

'Yes, I do. You know how I feel. I'm no fan of marriage, but I'm all for a stable relationship. Something terribly special, something precious and quite separate from my professional life. And now I have that.'

Den sat forward and swallowed some more brandy. 'Tell me something – why did you quote that bit of poetry at me?'

'Because it fitted,' Jan said. 'You had just made love to me in a very – um – urgent way. Then you seemed ashamed.'

Den nodded. 'I treated you like a one-off quickie. I shouldn't do that.'

'You should do what you feel like doing.' She kissed him again. 'It was honest, Den. That's all that matters. Tonight I was your whore. Last time you were timid

43

with me. Next time – who knows? We have variety, honesty. What's wrong with that?'

Den put down his glass. As Jan stood up he pushed the duvet aside and swung his feet out over the side of the bed. 'I don't want to go,' he sighed.

'But you have to.' Jan stepped close as he rose to his feet. 'Just remember, missing somebody is very sweet in its way, if you know for sure that you'll see them again.' Their bodies touched as he kissed her gently on the forehead. 'You're my special man, Denis Watts. And I'm your special woman, for as long as you want.'

Twenty-five minutes later, Den walked into the pub to find Detective Inspector Grazier waiting for him. From the policeman's expression it was clear he wasn't there to deliver good news. One glance at Angie confirmed she was in no chummy frame of mind, either. Den was back to his troubled life, the one full of traps and conflicts. He shivered involuntarily as the ghost of Jan's warmth left him. One day, he thought, he would drum up the will to make some big changes in this other life.

5

Ali Osman sidled across to the table where Robbie Wood was ogling a magazine. The picture that held his attention was of a girl almost as gross as himself, fifteen stone if she was a pound, wearing only a leer and her voluminous fat. Ali shook his head at the expanse of bloated pink. 'Bloody hell,' he murmured. 'That turns you on, does it?'

Robbie looked up. His small eyes had the intensity of an art-lover's. 'I reckon she's gorgeous.'

'Yeah, you would.' The man who spoke was sitting by the wall, his face halfway in shadow. He was Fred Kirk, a cowboy plumber who carried his own permanent atmosphere of gloom. 'Have you seen his motor, Ali? Green and cream, it is. Got big furry dice hanging on the windscreen, leopard-skin seat covers, noddin' dog on the back shelf, bumper stickers – the lot.' Fred made his fleeting version of a smile. 'You've got real taste, Robbie.'

'I've got a lot more than you,' Robbie said indignantly. He held up the magazine. 'Birds like this are an improvement on some of the slags you hang about with.' Robbie was able to say that freely, because it was well-known that Fred Kirk had no violence in him, apart from his vocal spite. 'Last one I saw, she was a right mess.' Robbie grinned up at Ali. 'She'd knockers on her the size of marbles an' a face like a jar of walnuts.'

'Shut it, fat man.' Fred stood up and strode impatiently to the door. It was a small room, an office at the back of Robbie's carpet shop. Fred made it to the door in three strides and stopped. 'Where the hell are them other blokes?'

'Den'll get here,' Ali said. 'He just has to square things with his missus.'

Fred grunted. 'I've seen her. I wouldn't mind squarin' a thing or two with her meself.' He looked at Robbie. 'What about the other one? You did tell him nine o'clock, didn't you?'

'Yeah.' Robbie looked at his watch. 'It's only five past. He's got a couple of deliveries to make. He won't be long.'

'Who is he anyway?' Ali enquired.

'Wally Simpson. He's a printer – raffle tickets, handbills, posters, that kind of thing.' The game had been arranged then re-arranged twice. Robbie's acquaintance was a last-minute replacement for a player who'd had to drop out. 'He's as good a poker man as the rest of us.'

Ali nodded, reflecting that Robbie's assumption about their similarity of talent was well out of line. Den was good and Ali fancied he was just as good himself, but Robbie and Fred were in the twerp league. They hadn't much grasp of the finer points of strategic play, their nerve was thin and when there was a decent pot on the table you could read their faces like outsize headlines. If this Simpson bloke was in their category the night would turn out to be a profitable walk-over.

Den turned up just as Robbie had decided to leaf through his book of beefy beauties for a second time.

'All right, mate?' Ali studied Den's expression. He detected some tension. 'No trouble gettin' away?'

'Of course I'd trouble gettin' away. I always do, don't I?'

Ali introduced Robbie and Fred. Den knew them faintly by sight. They shook hands and Den sat down immediately. 'Right then,' he said, rubbing his hands. 'Let's get to it, eh?'

'There's one to come yet,' Ali told him.

The tension returned to Den's face. He drummed his fingers and looked about the room for a moment, then he stood up again and stuck his hands in his pockets. 'Got anythin' to drink, have we?'

Robbie produced a bottle of whisky and gave them all a glass. While Fred returned glumly to his shady chair by the wall and Robbie fished another magazine out of the filing cabinet, Ali took Den aside.

'You're a bit agitated, mate,' he murmured. 'Not the best frame of mind for playin' cards, is it? What's up?'

'Not a lot, really.' Den made a face at the wall. 'Angie put up the usual barrage of bullshit about me always goin' off when the place is busy. An' of course she don't believe I'm off to no card game. So we had a ten-minute ding-dong an' when I'd finally shut her up, in strolls the Plod. Grazier. Know him?'

Ali nodded. 'He's such a bastard, even the other coppers have noticed it. You in some kind of trouble, then?'

'Looks like it.' Den lowered his voice. 'A while back I bought a load of fags off Tim Duffy. They turned out to be duty-frees. That was bad enough, but Grazier was prepared to believe I'd been turned over. Now it's got really serious. The code on the packet the police got off me was a giveaway. It corrcsponds with the batch serial on a load that was lifted out of a warehouse at Heathrow.'

'God almighty,' Ali said, trying to make it sound sympathetic.

'A lot of other stuff went in the same raid. Thousands of quid's worth. So the Law wants names. I'm bein' leaned on to remember where I got the fags. If I don't get me memory back, there's the distinct threat of a conspiracy charge.'

'Give them Duffy's name, then. He wouldn't think twice about shoppin' you, if he had to.'

Den shook his head slowly. 'It ain't that simple. I've been on to slimy little Tim already. After a bit of wafflin' he explained where *he* got the fags.' Den paused and rubbed his forehead, as if he was trying to drive out some corrosive knowledge. 'He was asked to handle the distribution by none other than Jock Clarke.'

Ali blinked. 'Christ. That's serious.'

'You can say that again. If the Law ever got on to Mad Jock about them fags, he'd start his cleansin' operation with Duffy an' then carve his way through anybody that had any dealin's with the warehouse gear.'

'So what are you goin' to do?'

'God knows. Grazier's been to see me twice now. Next time I've got to come up with somethin', or I'm in it right up past my hubcaps. He's not kiddin'. He never is.'

There was a tap on the side door and Robbie opened it. A tall man in a black zippered windcheater came in and nodded to the others. He was in his forties and had a face that looked too calm to be natural. As he unzipped his jacket Robbie made the introductions.

'Wally Simpson, lads. Wally, this is Fred, Ali and Den.'

Watching the man and feeling the brief, startling power of his handshake, Den decided that he might be called Wally, but there wasn't an ounce of the wally in this one. He was shrewd, calculating and self-possessed. His eyes made judgements about you and kept the findings secret. Tonight's game wasn't going to be the pushover Ali had predicted.

'Shall we all get ourselves settled then, gentlemen?' Robbie had adopted his salesman's voice as he pulled back the chairs and set three new packs of cards on the table. 'Draw poker as agreed. Variable limit by mutual consent.'

Den sat down and noticed that Wally Simpson chose to sit directly opposite. That kind of confrontation could harm Den's style in his present shaky emotional state.

'Here we go, then,' Robbie said brightly as he broke the seal on a deck of cards. 'To the victor the spoils, eh?'

Maybe I shouldn't have come, Den thought, watching the cold eyes across the table getting ready to read his mind.

Angie had a terrible dream that night. She dreamt she was standing in the bar, dressed in a pure silk dress. Her make-up was perfect, she had on her best rings and gold-rope chains and her mood was sparkling.

Opposite her, entranced by her appearance and hanging on her every word, a handsome young man was sipping a Pernod and nodding gently as she spoke. Angie had seen no one like him in her waking life. His hair was neat-clipped and impossibly blond, his skin had a light gold tan, he had sapphire eyes and his teeth, when he smiled, were like subtly serrated ivory. Suddenly he put down his glass, reached forward with one manicured finger and placed it on Angie's lips. Having silenced her, he then told her he adored her and wanted her to be his lover.

Then the dream began to change. As the blue of the young man's eyes grew darker with passion, the pub door swung open and Den walked in with his arm round a beautiful auburn-haired girl. She was much younger than Angie. She was also as improbably attractive as the dream man at the bar. Den led her to a table and they sat down. They seemed to be oblivious to Angie's presence. The girl giggled a lot and Den laughed the way he used to, openly, without roughness or bitterness, his face radiant with happiness.

At that point Angie didn't know how to feel. She glanced at her young man again. He was staring at Den's girl. Angie's heart tightened. She began to talk brightly again but the young man was ignoring her. He was still gazing across to where Den and his girl were holding each other and laughing intimately. Their heads were touching now and Angie felt a sudden flaring of jealousy. She took a deep breath, ready to shout at Den.

He stopped laughing suddenly and looked straight at her. His face took on a terrible frown, almost a look of revulsion. The girl was frowning too. They seemed more than shocked by the sight of Angie. They looked horrified. She turned and stared at herself in the mirror. The fine dress was still there, so was the twinkling jewellery, but Angie's face had changed. It was still her, but the make-up had gone and there were deep, fissured lines on her cheeks and around her sunken eyes. Her lips looked like two dried segments of orange and her teeth were hideously stained. She tried to scream but no sound came out.

She spun back to the bar and saw that Den and the girl were laughing again, but now they were laughing at her. As their sound grew they seemed to get further and further away, travelling to a distance as remote and cold as the gap that had grown between Den and Angie across the years. Soon there was no sign of them; all that remained was the harshening sound of their laughing.

Angie was choking on her shock and distress. She reached out and grasped her young man's shoulder, making him face her. She looked at him, imploring his sympathy, then realized it wasn't him. It was horrible old Reg Cox, and he was picking his nose again.

She woke up with a start. The room was dark and cold, but Angie could feel a sheen of sweat on her arms and body. As the awful dream receded she sat up, hearing a sound in the passage outside.

'Sharon? Is that you?'

There was no reply.

'Sharon?'

Silence. Angie got out of bed, trembling as she reached for the stick she always kept beside the night table. She tiptoed to the door and opened it a crack. Someone moved past the top of the stairs. Angie drew

51

the door an inch wider and saw Den go past, heading for his own room.

'Bloody hell!' Angie threw her door wide and strode out into the passage. 'You didn't half put the wind up me! What time is it, for God's sake?'

Den reached into his room and switched on the light. 'I told you I'd be late,' he said wearily.

'Yeah, well. Late usually means you'll be back with the milkman. This is the middle of the night.'

'The game finished early,' Den lied. For all he knew, the game would go on for hours yet. He had left because he had lost all his money, plus some he hadn't even taken with him.

'Tough luck, Denis.' Angie's heart was still thudding, partly from her fright, partly because of that dream. 'Next time you finish early with whatever it is you really do all night, walk round the streets until it gets light, will you?'

'Sorry if I interrupted your beauty sleep.' Den stared at her dully. 'It doesn't seem to have been doin' you much good, anyway.'

The dream flashed through Angie's head again. She saw them laughing at her, him and his girl, ridiculing her across the helpless, aching space. She suddenly wanted to cry. Why was it all pain with him, all hurt?

'Den . . .' Something broke in her, making her want to touch him, to touch any living soul for comfort. She moved towards him. 'Den, please . . .'

'It's late, Angie, as you've just been pointin' out. See you in the mornin'.'

Angie stopped. For a moment she stared at the dim-lit pattern on the carpet, taking a tight grip on herself, not letting him see how vulnerable she felt. They turned from each other finally, in silence, taking their solitary distress to their separate rooms.

Den closed the door and leaned on it. His head ached, his legs felt like lead, but he knew he wouldn't sleep. Not there, anyway. The Vic was too close to the centre of his miseries.

'Six hundred bleedin' quid,' he breathed.

It had happened so fast. Wally Simpson hadn't turned out to be such a great player, but what he lacked in tactics he made up for in nerve. Den, for his part, had been disastrously off form. He made blunders, simple mistakes even fat Robbie Wood wouldn't have made. To make matters worse there were those eyes of Simpson's, boring into him all the time, brightening occasionally with triumph as Den's bottle went and he made another blunder.

'What a soddin' life,' he groaned. He crossed and sat on the bed, his head drooping. His mind couldn't find peace. Every change of mental direction brought another pang. Grazier was out to scald him. Angie was playing merry hell with his nerves and his self-respect. On top of which he was down by six hundred pounds he couldn't afford to lose. Brewery bills were due, electricity too, and gas, plus a cartload of other costs that would be worry enough without the gambling loss and the other aggro. All he needed now was a spot check by the Customs and Excise.

He let his mind drift to his only hope of peace and temporary escape. He thought of Jan. He knew she was away for the weekend, but that didn't change the impulse to be near her. He would even settle for the chance to talk to her for a few minutes. Maybe she hadn't gone away after all, he thought. It had happened before, she'd had to change her plans for one reason or another. Feeling she was the one source of comfort he could turn to, Den got up, put out the light and crept downstairs to the telephone.

As he dialled he prayed, willing her to be at the other end. He stood with the receiver jammed to his ear, listening to the call tone. When it had run twelve times Den's hope began to sink. It rang three more times, and he decided to let it ring another four before he hung up.

Suddenly the tone stopped. After a split-second's confusion, Den realized the receiver had been picked up at the other end. He heard tired breathing along the line. He opened his mouth to whisper into the mouthpiece, then a man's voice spoke to him.

'Hello?' it said wearily. 'Who's there?'

Den gulped. 'Erm, what number is that, please?'

The man patiently told him the number. It was Jan's.

'Sorry,' Den said. 'I made a mistake.'

He put down the 'phone. Where there had been pain before, agony was beginning to swell. He put his hands over his face, hearing the voice again, the cultured accent. A man. A bloody *man!*

He let his hands drop to his sides and gazed ahead of him, seeing nothing, then he let out one soft, tearing groan. As the throb in his head got stronger, making it feel as if the bones would split apart, he grasped the rail and slowly climbed the stairs to his room.

6

It was said in Walford that Desmond Fine would buy
anything off you, but nobody in the district had ever
known him to sell anything. As far as anyone knew,
Desmond had no business premises, no warehouse,
not even an office, yet he did a steady trade and he
always looked prosperous.

There were a number of theories about how the
man operated. The most popular notion – which was
shared by the police – was that Desmond did his selling
outside of London, through a network of specialist
contacts. If he was a crook, though, no policeman or
informer had ever been able to prove it. Desmond's
record was as spotless as the white silk shirts he always
wore.

Physically, Desmond was an ordinary-looking,
slightly overweight East End Jewish man, aged somewhere in his fifties. The most noticeable thing about
him, especially to someone seeing him for the first
time, was his right hand. On the second, third and
fourth fingers he wore a total of seven rings. Their
digital permutations varied from day to day. That hand
was worth a fortune; on mounts and bands of gold and
platinum there were seed pearls, sapphires, a ruby and
a pair of matched diamonds that flashed vividly when
Desmond waved his arm, which he always did when
he was conducting a deal.

Walking along Bridge Street that cold Monday morning, Desmond had his showpiece hand dug deep in the pocket of a dark blue cashmere overcoat. He wore a bright yellow scarf wound loosely around his neck and his balding scalp was protected by a sporty blue cap. In his left hand he carried a hand-stitched black leather attaché case.

'There he goes,' Pete Beale muttered to Kathy as Desmond passed the fruit stall. 'King of the manor. If I'd a tenth the gelt he's got, I'd be livin' in the Bahamas. Beats me why he stays round here.'

'He does it to make all that gelt you're on about,' Kathy said. 'He wouldn't do a lot of trade in the Bahamas, or up West for that matter. He's where his livin' is.'

'I suppose so.' Pete lobbed a bruised apple into a box under the barrow. 'Just the same, you'd think at his age he'd start enjoyin' the dough. Far as I can tell he don't go out much, he hasn't got a car an' he lives in a pokey little house over on Firth Road.'

'No women in his life, neither,' Kathy said. She watched Desmond enter The Vic by the corner door. 'Maybe money's all he wants. Some people love it for its own sake.'

Pete shrugged. 'Maybe *I* would. I've never had any long enough to find out.'

Inside The Vic Ethel was tidying away her cleaning things as the first customer came in. She recognized him at once and smiled broadly. 'Mornin', Mr Fine. Somebody'll see to you directly. Den's just popped down to the cellar.'

Desmond nodded and put his case on the bar. He climbed on to a stool, being careful not to crush the

56

tail of his coat. As Ethel disappeared through the doorway behind the bar Angie came through from the back. She smiled at the customer too, though not as warmly as Ethel had.

'Cold mornin' again,' she said chirpily. 'What'll it be?'

Desmond drummed his ringed fingers as he decided. 'I think I'll have an orange juice.'

'One orange juice it is.'

Angie took the cap off a bottle and poured the drink into a stemmed glass. Beneath the veil of her eyelashes she was watching Desmond, gauging his businesslike manner. On the odd occasions when he dropped in for a drink – never more than one, and always a whisky – he never sat like that, all upright with his bag in front of him. The only other time he had sat that way, as far as she could remember, was when Den had got in a financial scrape and needed help. That was two years ago, and she believed Desmond Fine had ordered an orange juice on that occasion, too.

'There we are, then.' She gave him his drink and picked up the pound note he had already put on the bar. As she turned to the till Den appeared. She noticed the way his face changed when he saw the solitary customer. Trouble again, she thought grimly.

'Hello there, Mr Fine.' Den said it with hollow affability. 'How have things been?'

Desmond's hand fluttered, making the diamonds wink. 'As well as can be expected. It's an uphill struggle. How about yourself?'

Angie handed Desmond his change and glared at Den. 'Always uphill in this trade too,' she said. 'Isn't it, Den?'

'Oh, things have been worse,' Den said lightly. 'We do as well as any pub round here, I reckon.' He looked at Angie, folding his arms defensively. 'If you want to go off an' get your shoppin', I'll take care of things here.'

'There's no rush,' she snapped.

'Suit yourself.'

For the next five minutes Angie made Den roast as she tidied the already tidy shelves, checked the optics and went round straightening beer mats and ashtrays on the bar and tables. Den pretended to be checking the till, glancing occasionally at Desmond, who was making his drink last by taking microscopic sips every minute or so.

Finally Angie announced that she was going out to the shops. Before she left, she gave Den one more hard look. It was a glower of warning, serving him notice that she knew there was some new trouble on his overloaded plate, and that she would be adding more when she got him on his own.

'Sorry about that,' Den said as she left. 'It would have been easier if I could've come an' seen you somewhere.'

'This is the way I do business,' Desmond said simply. 'You call me, I come.'

'Yeah,' Den sighed, 'I know.'

'So.' Desmond folded his hands on his case. 'I'm here. What can I do for you?'

'Same as before. I need a few readies . . .'

Desmond smiled delicately. 'I'm not a money-lender, as you know. What have you got on offer?'

Den chewed his lip for a moment. 'It depends. See, I'm tryin' to raise seven, eight hundred. But I don't want to strip all me assets in the process. What kind of things do you like buyin' best?'

Desmond smiled at the naïve approach. 'Normally, as with you the last time, somebody comes right out and offers me something. If I want it, I'll pay a fair price.'

Den remembered what a pain it had been to part with his Rolex watch and the solid gold cufflinks he'd had since he was twenty. The money Desmond gave him was hardly fair, but it got him out of a tough spot.

'Well, I've a camera, an' there's this.' Den pushed back his cuff and undid his watch. He handed it to Desmond.

'Very nice.' The jewelled fingers waved around a little as he held the watch, hefting it, making a valuation. 'Breitlings are worth a bit of money of course . . .' He winced fleetingly, making it look like regret. 'If it had been a Vacheron Constantin, though, or one of the better Cartiers . . .'

Den waited, watching Desmond's sharp eyes check the elaborate watch for scratches and dents. He wouldn't find any. Den had treated the instrument with obsessive care for seven months, ever since Jan gave it to him. When Angie had asked about it he told her he got it cheap from somebody in the bar. A few days ago it would have been a possession so precious he would never have parted with it, whatever the emergency. Now he felt a little differently. The watch threw back thoughts of treachery whenever he checked the time. Even so, he would hate losing it.

Desmond laid the watch on his case, satisfied that it was in immaculate condition. 'What about the camera?'

'I'll get it.'

Den went to the cupboard under the stairs and dug out a shiny leather holdall from beneath four packets of bar towels. He took it to the bar and opened it.

'Top quality gear,' he murmured. 'An' before you ask, I've got all the documents for that as well as the watch.'

'Mmm.' Desmond lifted out the spotless Canon body and its three lenses, lining them up on his case beside the watch. 'It all looks brand new, I must say.'

Den nodded. It was less than a year old and he had put only one roll of film through it. He knew it was one of the best cameras in the world, but it had been a crazy purchase, a complete waste of money. Jan had encouraged him to take up the hobby as part of her programme to widen his interests. She had recommended the Canon and helped him choose the lenses. Judging from the results he'd produced, Den reckoned he could have saved himself five hundred quid and bought an Instamatic instead.

'Yes, it's in mint condition,' Desmond announced when he had finished fiddling with the camera and firing its shutter a couple of times. 'Again, though, if it had been a top-of-range Nikon, or better still a Leica . . .'

'How much?'

Desmond's hand fluttered. The rings winked. He frowned at his attache case, as if it might be telling him what to say. 'For both the watch and the camera . . . Well.' He fell silent, his lips clamped.

'Yeah?'

'Four hundred.'

Den stared at him. 'They're worth a lot more than that, for God's sake . . .'

'It's the best I can do,' Desmond said. His voice sounded infinitely sad. 'It's the top ends of the ranges that hold their value. Good as these items are – indeed they're excellent – I have to take depreciation into account.'

Den sighed. 'You wouldn't go to four-fifty?' He knew Desmond wouldn't. The hand had stopped waving so the dealing was over.

'Four hundred.' It was as final as a jail sentence.

Den took the money and handed over the goods. When Desmond had gone he felt a sudden, intense wave of shame. He realized he had jettisoned a huge chunk of his relationship with Jan. That watch had been a gift, the most special gift she had given him. The camera was a symbol, however misguided, of her hopes for him, of her interest in bringing out his talents. He had sold them both because he'd lost money at cards. It was no use thinking of how she'd betrayed him. He was still a bastard for doing what he had just done.

A lot of customers drifted in and out during the next hour, keeping Den busy, holding his mind just off the edge of his misery, his self-loathing and worry. Every time the door opened he expected it to be Inspector Grazier, come for his showdown. During most of a fretful Sunday and halfway through a sleepless night, Den had tried to think of something to get him off the hook with Grazier. But too much else had interfered with his concentration. He had no idea what he would tell the Inspector.

Angie got back at noon. In keeping with their policy of never letting disputes show in the bar, she communicated her displeasure to Den in spurts, delivered between bouts of smiling conversation and joking banter with the customers.

'You're a born loser,' she managed to tell him during a lull. They stood at the bottom of the stairs, glaring at each other. 'What did you flog Mr Bigbucks this time? Half me clothes? Our daughter's cassette player? Maybe you could've got a few bob on the food processor . . .'

'Just can it, Ange,' he warned her. 'One of these days you'll lay on the acid a bit too hard an' – '

'Yeah?' She stuck her face close to his. 'An what? You talk big an' walk big for a worm, don't you? Just what emergency brought that bloke here this mornin'? Eh?'

'A cash-flow problem,' Den muttered, trying to hold her stare. 'Nothin' that couldn't be handled.'

Angie stood back, hands on hips, assessing him. 'What kind of a man are you? You've got your life organized like a bomb site.'

'Angie, pack it in . . .'

'All that chat you used to hand me about gettin' a properly run, profitable up-market business goin' one day – since when does a spiv like you qualify for anythin' halfway respectable or up-market?'

Den tried to cut her off, but Angie ranted on.

'You spend your days staggerin' from one balls-up to the next,' she hissed, 'pretendin' to the world you're a big shot when you're nothin' but a waste of bloody space. Know somethin'?' She shoved her face close to his again. 'You're a mug an' a bum an' I'm sick to my stomach with you!'

Suddenly, watching her stride off to serve a customer, Den felt defeated. Somewhere in her slanging she had struck a chink that led all the way to his core. He had felt bad since Saturday, but not so bad as this. It hurt, worse than anything he could remember.

At twenty past five, with the bar empty and Angie occupied upstairs with Sharon, Den finished bottling up and went to the telephone. It was not a call he looked forward to making, but it had to be done. Some vestige of self-respect, of self-esteem, had to be rescued. He lifted the receiver and dialled. Jan answered at once.

'It's me,' he said huskily.

'Darling!' She sounded cheerful and breathless. 'I just got in this minute. How are you?'

'I'm fit.' He swallowed. 'Have a good weekend, did you?'

'So-so,' Jan said. 'Duty visits are always a mixed bag. My father's in good spirits at the moment, though, so it had its bright spots.'

'How terribly interestin'.'

Jan was silent for a moment. 'Den? What's up?'

'Nothin' much. It's just that I phoned you the other night, very late . . .'

'But I told you I'd be away.'

He nodded at the receiver. 'Even so. I was feelin' a bit low, I thought I'd like to talk for a bit, – you know, the way we liked to do sometimes. I made a bad move though, didn't I?'

Again she hesitated before saying anything. 'Den what is it? Are you cross with me or something?'

'Cross?' He cleared his throat, trying to stop the tremor that was entering his voice. 'I think bloody mad's a better expression, Jan.'

'What?'

'You heard. Mad, bloody mad.'

'Come on then,' she said stiffly. 'Out with it. What's wrong?'

'You're wrong, that's what. Who was the bloody bloke that answered your phone?'

'What night are you talking about?'

He groaned. 'For Christ's sake Jan, don't play games. I'm on to you an' that's that. I know what you're up to. I should have known how many faces you'd got.'

'Den!'

'I called Saturday night, nearer Sunday mornin', an' some feller with marbles in his mouth answered the blower.'

'I see.' Jan's voice had suddenly become cold and distant. 'That would be Nigel. Remember I told you about him? Nigel Russell. My cousin.'

The memory exploded in Den's head. He felt himself turn cold. The anger drained away as a fresh wave of shame hit him. He wet his lips, wondering what to say. 'Listen, Jan . . .' he stammered. 'You can imagine what I thought . . .'

'I'm afraid I can, even though you know Nigel often uses this place when he's in town and I'm away.'

Den had to stop himself from groaning. 'Look, I forgot, that's all . . .'

'Forgetting's no sin,' Jan said. 'But your sordid accusation is.'

'I wasn't accusin' you.'

'Oh yes you were,' she snapped. 'Is that the measure of the faith you put in me? Has nothing I said about the way I feel meant anything to you at all?' He heard

64

her draw in a steadying breath. 'Thank you, Den. Thank you for showing me how shallow you are. It's not often somebody does me a favour as big as that.'

'Jan, please . . .'

The line clicked and went dead.

Den gaped at the silent receiver in his hand, then at the mirror above the telephone. He saw his wide, unbelieving eyes, his pale cheeks, his half-open mouth. What he saw, in total, was a face that sickened him far more than it could ever repel Jan, or Angie, or anyone else.

7

During the Tuesday morning break at school, Sharon Watts told her best mate, Michelle Fowler, that she believed her father was cracking up.

'I know he's a bit strange at the best of times, but what's happenin' now is really freaky.' Sharon rolled her eyes, as children do when adult oddities bewilder them. 'Twice last night – *twice* – he walked into the kitchen, forgot what he'd come in for and walked out again. Then about midnight, I woke up an' heard him groanin' in the livin' room.'

Michelle was a year older than Sharon, therefore she regarded herself as being miles wiser. 'That don't mean he's goin' loopy,' she told her friend dismissively. 'He could be sickenin' for somethin'. Maybe he's gettin' the 'flu.'

'Nah.' Sharon shook her head firmly. 'It's all in his nut. This mornin' I looked into the bar to say cheerio, an' he was stood there just starin' across at the windows. His eyes were all glassy an' creepy lookin'. When I went up to him, told him I was goin' an' kissed his cheek, he turns on me all of a sudden an' says "What?" From the look on his face you'd think I'd pulled a knife on him.' She leaned on the wall and sighed. 'What with Mum on the drink again, an' him goin' round the bend, I'm startin' to wonder if I should nip across an' have a word with Dr Legg. There's no sayin' where it'll all lead.'

'Don't be silly.' Michelle nibbled on her sandwich, considering what she had been told. 'Your mum only hits the bottle when she's feelin' a bit low. She ain't an alcoholic or nothin' like that. Your dad's in business an' that's got a lot of worries attached to it. He's likely got a problem. When he sorts it out he'll be all right.'

Sharon wasn't willing to accept any ordinary explanation. 'You don't have to live with it. Her stumblin' about the place, him wanderin' around like a moanin' zombie . . .'

'Don't blow it all up out of shape, Shar. Your parents aren't any weirder than most.'

'You reckon?' Sharon lowered her head like a conspirator. She beckoned Michelle closer, even though there was nobody else near them. 'Normal married people sleep together, don't they?'

Michelle shrugged. 'Who knows? Books an' films tell you one thing, but for all we know real life might be totally different.' It was necessary, Michelle felt, to contradict Sharon as often as she could. Otherwise, the girl was apt to turn every ordinary event into high drama. 'I'll bet a lot of men an' women can't stick sleepin' two to a bed.'

'Your mum an' dad do, don't they?'

'They've got no flamin' choice. There's five of us livin' in that rabbit hutch.'

Sharon sniffed. 'I still don't think it's natural, husbands an' wives havin' different bedrooms.'

Michelle didn't think it was natural either, but that was beside the point. 'You really want to paint them black, don't you?' she said. 'They're just a couple with all the ups an' downs other couples have.'

'I'm paintin' them the way they are,' Sharon insisted.

'I bet my real parents aren't people like that.' Being an adopted child was one of Sharon's excuses for claiming, often, that she was underprivileged – other girls lived in proper houses, other girls had real parents. 'When you come to think of it, people as odd as them two shouldn't be allowed to adopt kids, should they?'

This was beginning to bore Michelle. 'There's nothin' up with your folks,' she snapped. 'It's you that's a bit touched, if you ask me.'

'Oh yeah?'

'Yeah.' Michelle saw another friend and waved to catch her attention. 'Look, I'll see you in a bit, Shar. I want to talk to Doreen about somethin'.' She picked up her bag and walked away briskly.

Watching her go, Sharon hunched her shoulders and slid down the wall until she was crouching. Sitting like that she felt safer. It was the way she sat at home when they were having a row. It was the way she curled up in bed when she heard her mother crying in the night.

'Nobody wants to understand,' she murmured, feeling her self-pity swell. The things she told Michelle about her home life never seemed to convey the essence of her insecurity or her occasional fear. It was nothing she could describe; perhaps Michelle would understand better if she knew that going home to The Vic each day, Sharon was more anxious than she ever felt about going to school.

Inspector Grazier put his shoulders against the side of the fruit machine, crossed his ankles and slid his hands into his trouser pockets. It was a well-rehearsed pose, his own notion of looking like a casual but lethal threat.

'Now then,' he said to Den. 'Have the clouds cleared from your memory?'

Den pocketed his own hands to conceal their tremor. This encounter had loomed in his mind for so long, it was almost a relief that the moment had arrived.

'Look, Inspector, it's tricky. I mean, I don't want to drop a name that might be wrong. I don't want to go makin' trouble for somebody that don't deserve it.'

'If you name an innocent party,' Grazier said slowly, 'he's got nothing to worry about. He'll be cleared.' He smiled at Den, relishing his nervousness. 'Now come along. I'm a busy man. Where did you get those cigarettes?'

'I honestly can't remember.'

'Oh dear.'

Den struggled to keep his expression of sincere bafflement. 'Honest to God, Inspector, if I could help you I would.'

'Dear oh dear me . . .' Grazier shook his head sorrowfully. 'You know what this'll mean, of course.'

'But I – '

'It'll mean you go down on the sheet as being party to a major theft, and when the time for prosecutions comes . . .' Grazier paused, as if the rest was too awful to mention.

'Aw come on, Inspector,' Den stared at him, his eyes pleading. 'You know I'm not a villain.'

Grazier's face hardened. 'I know nothing of the sort.'

Den pictured a courtroom, a hard-eyed judge, a prison yard; then he pictured big Mad Jock Clarke.

There was no contest between the images. He would sooner do a stretch than even hint that the Scotsman was involved.

'I'm off,' the Inspector said abruptly, He straightened up and took his hands out of his pockets. 'Wheels have to be set in motion. I may be back later.'

'What for?' Den asked dismally.

'There could be some justification for making a search of these premises.' Grazier buttoned his jacket and turned towards the door. 'We won't do that without letting your area manager know, of course.' That extra blow made Den sag visibly, he noticed. 'Everything'll be done by the book, have no fear of that.'

Den looked along the pub, finding it too small to contain his desolation. 'Hell's bells, Inspector, is there any need to go to these lengths? I mean we're only talkin' about a few fags . . .'

Grazier tilted his head haughtily. 'We're talking about a crime, Mr Watts. A crime I'm going to investigate thoroughly until I've solved it. And when I've got my villains gathered in, I'll make out a prosecution case that'll be just as thorough.' He pulled open the door, gave Den one final hard look, then left.

Den looked round the pub again, imagining what would happen if the area manager got wind of a police investigation. He would move in with his troops and sift the dust. Every fiddle, large and small, would be pinpointed and duly recorded. Brewery managements, when they set their minds to it, could crucify a landlord.

'Well?' Angie had appeared from the back. 'How did it go?'

Den blinked at her. 'How do you think? The law's gettin' all set to slice off my head and ram it down my neck.' By now, he took Angie's disapproval and contempt for granted. He tried not to look at her as he stepped nearer the bar. 'Grazier's tryin' to get the brewery rolled into it now.'

'Bloody hell,' Angie groaned. 'Do you realize – '

'Yes, Ange,' Den interrupted, 'I do understand what it'll mean. An' I also know what a heap of shit you think I am for bringin' all this down on us, but there you are, it's happened.'

Angie gripped the handle of a beer pump as if she might want to tear it off and club Den with it. 'There's no sayin' what they'll come up with.'

Den went behind the bar and began drying some glasses. At least, he thought, nobody would find any contraband fags. Two days before, he had destroyed the other boxes of duty-frees out in the yard. It had been a nightmare. Instead of tearing open the cartons and scattering the contents before he tried to burn them, he had simply dumped the lot in a dustbin full of paraffin-soaked newspapers. It had been a spectacular blaze, but when it died down the cartons were still more or less intact. They were also very hot and Den scorched his fingers trying to rip them apart. In the end, after ten minutes of struggling, he managed to liberate all the cigarettes and pour more paraffin on them. This time they did burn, but they made a huge pall of smoke that attracted the attention of a passing constable. He had only grudgingly accepted Den's explanation that he was burning some old oily rags.

'Will you be able to cope here?' Angie said. 'I want to go out to the shops.'

Den nodded. 'Carry on.'

When she had gone, he served two customers then went straight to the telephone. He dialled the number of the store where Jan worked and asked for her extension. He cleared his throat as he heard her answer.

'Jan love, it's me . . .'

'I asked you not to call me here,' she snapped. 'Or at home.' Her voice was cold and hostile. 'I'm very busy. And besides, I've nothing to say to you.'

'But Jan, you've got to give me a chance to explain . . .'

'I haven't *got* to do anything where you're concerned. Goodbye.' The line clicked sharply and she was gone.

Den slammed down the receiver.

'Oi! is this place a self-service now, or what?'

He turned and saw Pete Beale at the bar.

'I've just popped in for a quick one, mate.' Pete smiled brightly, then he noticed Den's expression. 'What's up? Bad news?'

'My whole bloody life's bad news,' Den muttered, coming to the bar. 'What can I get you?'

Pete asked for a pint of lager. He watched thoughtfully as Den pulled it. 'I saw that Grazier comin' out of here a couple of minutes ago. Havin' problems in that direction, are you?'

Den nodded. 'There an' elsewhere. Every direction you can think of.' He put the drink in front of Pete. 'I must have insulted a gipsy or somethin'.'

Pete looked along the bar to make sure no one else was listening. He leaned closer to Den. 'Speakin' as your mate,' he said. 'I reckon if you sorted out your domestic set-up, you'd be well on the way to gettin' straight all round.' He winked. 'Me an' Kath have got our troubles, lots of them, but we always keep the home front in order. It's a solid base to work from, Den. Gives you the strength to tackle whatever comes along.'

Den frowned at him. 'Who said there's anythin' wrong between me an' Angie?'

'Well, you don't need to be too smart to notice things like that . . .'

'Christ.' Den stared at the bar. 'On top of all the other crap I've got to cope with, I'm bein' handed marriage guidance across the bar.'

'Don't take it like that, mate . . .'

'It's the only way I *can* take it. I don't need this, Pete. What I need is answers to a load of problems, not mealy-mouthed advice about how to run my marriage.'

Pete shrugged. 'Sorry I spoke.' He picked up his pint and took it to a table.

Den went through to the back and stood at the bottom of the stairs, directionless, wondering what to do with himself. The spurt of outrage he had shown Pete had been the dregs of his resistance. He felt, suddenly, that everything was falling through and he could do nothing about it. This was the big one, the catastrophe he had always suspected beyond the horizon. It was coming at him like a bull and he was stuck in its path.

There was a sudden, cruelly tender memory of Jan, bending over him and smiling, soothing his cares with one gentle, stroking hand. That was gone, all his peace of mind and physical security, all his hope. He put his hands to his eyes and sighed against the palms. What could he do, he wondered bleakly.

An answer came at once, cold and clear. He could let go, just let it all happen and try to feel nothing. Or he could fight.

He turned and gazed through at the bar. His Uncle Archie had once told him that nothing was unavoidable except death. It was a notion Den liked, although he had never seriously tested it. Maybe now was the time. Facing up to his problems wasn't an enticing idea, but it seemed a lot better than just letting his life disintegrate.

As he went back to the bar he decided he would start on the home front, just like Pete had suggested. He was pretty sure, after all – in fact if he faced it he was certain – that his affair with Jan was over. He would have to accept that loss. While he was getting over the pain, he could put some spadework into his marriage. It would be a start.

8

So much of life's real pleasures – such as good-looking men, a bit of fun and a few giggles – was down to timing. Angie always said. She reckoned most of the memorable events in her life had been the result of purest timing on her part. The day years ago when she decided to have her first little fling (or a bit on the side, as Den would have put it), she had employed timing to manoeuvre herself into the right spot at the right moment, then by swift stages she had used her talent for timing to bring about a string of seeming coincidences that her lover believed, later, had been the signs of fate.

'Good timin's more important to a woman than her figure or her make-up,' Angie had once told Kathy. 'If you're built like Dolly Parton an' dressed like Lady Di, but you've got no timin', you just won't have as much jollies as a girl who has, whatever she looks like.'

Den's dismal timing in bed had been a source of unhappiness to Angie in the early days when they actually slept together. His lousy timing in everything, in fact, was a constant aggravation to his wife. On Wednesday morning, during an especially busy time in the bar, he demonstrated that shortcoming yet again.

'I've been thinkin',' he said casually, reaching across Angie to pull a pint.

'Don't strain nothin',' she snapped. 'Thinkin's dangerous with a head like yours.'

'No, seriously . . .'

'Come on, Den!' Arthur Fowler yelled. 'I've only ten minutes to get that down me!'

'Right right, hold your water.' Den swung the slopping pint from under the tap and banged it down in front of Arthur. 'Next time, send any urgent orders to me in advance. I'll see the drink's waitin' for you when you get here.' He took the money and threw it in the till. As Angie came past with a tray of glasses he tried to tackle her again. 'What it is, love,' he said, 'I thought maybe we – '

'Den! Not now, for God's sake. I'm up to me armpits in orders here an' I'm doin' sums at the same time.' The frosty stiffness left her face as she beamed at a group by the end of the bar. 'Here we are then,' she said brightly. 'Two pound eighty, please.'

Den waited until she took the cash and handed over the change. 'What I had in mind,' he said, 'was goin' up West an' havin' a slap-up dinner. You know, somethin' dead special, the full works.'

Angie stopped with a fresh pint glass in each hand. 'Eh?'

'Dinner, love. Up West.'

'What – you an' me?' She made the notion sound ridiculous.

'Why not?'

She put one glass on the bar and began filling the other. 'It's a bit like a snake invitin' a mongoose out for a stroll.' Her eyes narrowed. 'What're you up to?'

'Nothin'.' Lately, he felt he was always trying to look innocent and hurt at the same time. 'I'm not up to anythin'. I just think it'd be nice if you an' me could get out on our own an' try to rekindle some of that old magic – '

'I'd like that pint before closin' time, if it's all the same to you, darlin'.' The face of the man waiting by the bar resembled a malignant bun. The raisin-like eyes ran a swift check of Angie's bosom and hips. 'A fit girl like you should be able to work faster'n that.' He nudged his mate, a lookalike in a donkey jacket and greasy cap. They both sniggered without a trace of humour.

'Mind your gob, pal.' Den's neck shot out a clear inch from his collar as he leaned across the bar. 'If you don't like the service, take your street patter an' high-fashion gear out of here an' go to The Lion. They don't mind servin' gorillas down there.'

'Den!' Angie hissed, simultaneously flashing her smile at the two customers. 'Don't pay him no mind,' she chortled. 'He's been actin' strange all mornin'.' She glanced at Den. 'Very strange, as it happens.'

Den let time pass, feeling it was safer to get off the ragged-edged tack before he raised the matter again. Eventually a lull came up and he cornered her.

'What do you say, Ange? Maybe a wine bar first, then din-dins, with candlelight an' all the other schmaltz?'

Angie stared at him, her eyes flicking sharply to left and right, trying to read the motive behind his wide eyes and fixed smile. 'Whatever for?'

'To cancel all the bad stuff that's behind us. I think a fresh start's called for. Don't you?'

'I think a bloody miracle's called for, Den, but I

don't think anythin' you an' me can do is gonna work it.'

Den swallowed. 'We could give it a try.'

In spite of her annoyance about his timing and the strong suspicion that this could be some sort of sneaky diversion, Angie had to admit that something in her was touched. He looked so sincere. Maybe he *was* stricken with a need to get the marriage back on the rails, rusty as they were. Angie's preoccupation for the past several days had been their plight, the ghastly prospect of ruin at the hands of the police and the brewery. She had shut her mind to the actual consequences, to the terrible aftermath of having all they'd worked for taken away. The simple, vivid thought of it happening had been enough to keep her on the brink of panic. Den's proposition, daft as it was, felt like a balm on her chafed nerves. On top of that, it softened her aching certainty that fate had put the thumbs-down on her ever getting it together with Jimmy Solomon.

'I don't know, Den . . .'

'Where's the harm?'

'We'd most likely just start fightin' again,' she muttered. 'We can do that here for nothin', instead of spendin' all kinds of money in a restaurant.'

Den leaned close to her and touched her hand. 'Come on. I really mean it, I want us to try for a bit of sunshine in our lives.'

'You'd never notice it through all these clouds,' she said stubbornly. She stared at him again. He still looked sincere. She wondered about the other woman. Was that over? Or was it still on, and he was trying to put an end to the relationship?

78

'Saturday night,' Den said firmly. 'I'll get it booked. All you've got to say is OK.'

She sighed. 'Who'd look after the pub?'

'Kath. Good as gold, she is. An' the new part-timer's built like an ox, which'll keep the punters in line – an' he could use the extra money.' Den spread his hands. 'No problem. Just give me the nod, love.'

Angie made a show of grudging surrender. 'Oh, all right. It'll take me mind off things for an hour or two, I suppose.'

Something happened then that puzzled Angie. Den's smile widened, he glanced along the bar and then his face suddenly stiffened with foreboding. He turned very pale.

'Den?'

He was still looking at the far end of the bar.

'What is it?'

'Christ,' he groaned.

Angie turned and looked. There was a big man standing with one broad hand on the curve of the bar. He was dressed like a solicitor, but his face would have looked more at home above a wrestler's leotard.

'Who's he?' The features looked familiar, although Angie was sure she hadn't seen the man before. Then it dawned on her; he looked a bit like Kirk Douglas, with the refinements cut off. The firm, down-turned mouth and pale blue eyes were like a shorthand message about trouble. 'Den? I'm askin' you – who is he?'

'Jock Clarke,' Den breathed.

'What?' Angie looked shocked. '*Mad* Jock Clarke?'

'That's him.'

'He looks like he wants to talk to you.' Angie remembered the stories. A man had been thrown into a cement mixer; another one had lost an ear; an off-track bookie had had his hand nailed to the fence on the corner where he did business. 'Jesus Den, you've not got yourself rolled up with him, have you?'

'Nah.' Den's voice was a croak. 'I'll see what he wants.'

It was like the confrontation of fate and one of its victims, the stony solidity of big Jock on one side of the bar, the near boneless approach of Den on the other.

'Mornin',' Den squeaked. His smile wouldn't work. 'What can I get you?'

'Den Watts?' The man's eyes constricted to two ice-blue slits.

'That's me, yes.' Den cleared his throat noisily and clasped his hands in front of him. 'It's, ah, Mr Clarke, isn't it? I believe I've seen you around.'

'Ye might have.' The man's other hand joined the one resting on the bar, the knuckles bulging like skin-coated ballbearings. 'I'd like a word with ye.' He turned and pointed. 'Over there, where it's a bit private.'

Den went round the bar and followed his visitor to the corner table. They sat down opposite each other, Clarke lowering his bulk on to the creaky leather padding, Den making do with a stool.

'Now.' The massive hands met, hesitated, then clasped on the table. 'Before ah say anythin', Mr Watts, ah want yer word that this wee talk never took place.'

'Of course,' Den said hastily. 'When it comes to the old confidentiality, I'm a graveyard.'

Clarke's lips moved in something that might have

been a smile. 'Graveyard's an, eh, *appropriate* word, as it happens. Ah hate havin' ma heels dogged wi' things ah've said in the past – know what ah mean?'

Den hoped his gulp wasn't too loud. 'Yeah, I get you.'

'Right.' Clarke's head sank down a fraction, leaving his shoulders stolidly where they were. 'Ah'm led to understand you've had words wi' a certain arsehole by the name of Grazier. Is that right?'

Den nodded as the fear took a tight grip on his heart.

'He's no kind of a man, that one,' Clarke rasped. 'At the school ah went to in Glasgow, he'd have been the kind of kid that would get the Chinese burn every day, twice at least.' He hesitated, his eyes going distant as he pictured it. 'Not the sort of person to do business with – not that any scuffer is, mind you.'

'Mr Clarke – '

'Call me Jock. Even ma enemies call me that.'

Den gulped again. 'Jock. About what I said to Grazier, I didn't drop nobody in it nor anythin' like that . . .'

'Who said you did?'

'Well, nobody, but – '

'Just listen,' Clarke said slowly, 'then digest, then file away for good.' He looked to right and left, his face a challenge to anyone who fancied getting nearer. He fixed his gaze on Den again. 'See, I'm not a complicated person, Mr Watts. I get on wi' my business an' as far as possible I let other folk get on wi' theirs. What gets on my tits though, to put it bluntly, is men that'll do business with me, then talk about it to the wrong people – people like Grazier.'

81

Den was nodding, knowing he was doing it too rapidly. 'You've got my word, Jock, nothin' passed between him an' me that could do you the least bit of harm . . .'

'Ah think you said somethin' to that effect already. Ah'm not accusin' you. Ah'm here to put you in the picture.' The big head lowered another fraction. So did the voice. 'In the course of his inquiries, it seems, the man Grazier spoke to Tim Duffy – you're familiar with the weasel in question, of course?'

'Yeah.' Den's heart was still fluttering. He glanced round and saw Angie staring at him anxiously. 'I've come across him.'

'A right little shit,' Clarke pronounced gravely. 'Still, nature does that to some folk. Ah suppose they can't help it. Anyhow, Duffy somehow let it slip the other day that he might have had some dealin's with me lately. Next thing I know, Grazier's round at my place, askin' questions about some cigarettes an' other stuff.' Now the smile was real, a mark of something accomplished. 'I told him to bugger off, mind you, an' that was the end of the matter.'

Den's surprise overcame his anxiety for a moment. 'Grazier? You told him to move along?'

'Oh, aye.'

'An' he went?'

Clarke nodded once. 'Like a dog with its arse on fire.' One eye did a slow-motion wink. 'That was after I'd explained my deep learnin' on the subject of his nasty arrangements with certain drug-pushers, of course. An' I threw in a serious premonition I had about his health – the health of his backbone, to be precise – just to see him firmly on his way.' Clarke released a laugh like the bark of a deranged Alsatian. 'It was just mah luck they sent one of the Filth I'd got somethin' on, eh?'

Den was being assailed with awe, lingering terror and curiosity. At that moment curiosity was in the lead. 'What about Duffy?' he ventured.

'He's been attended to. What's the word for it, now?' Clarke screwed up his face in concentration. 'Oh, aye.' His features cleared. '*Chastised*, that's what he's been.'

Den wet his lips and nodded.

'In the process of clearin' up this bit of unpleasantness,' Clarke went on, 'I questioned another copper or two, in a casual sort of way . . .' Now his face changed. He looked at Den with open admiration. There was no mistaking it. 'What with Duffy's story, an' what I got off the law, I gather you were under a lot of pressure from Grazier to name names. I believe you could have dropped a couple – mine included. But you didn't.'

Den couldn't fill the momentary silence between them. He had never known relief like this. It was like having a spiritual transplant.

'I appreciate that, Mr Watts. If things had gone the other way, you might have got sent down for a stretch. You must have known that.'

Den managed to nod again.

'So.' One big hand unclasped from the other and slid across the table, its fingers extended. 'In the event, it wouldn't have mattered if you'd fingered me. But it's nice to meet a man that wouldn't, not even to save himself.'

Den took the hand and let it shake his. There was

no gain in reflecting that his loyalty towards Walford's own Dutch Schultz had been the result of purest fear. In that instant he felt no less than honoured. And cleansed.

Jock Clarke withdrew his hand and stood up. 'Ah'll not forget it, Mr Watts.'

Den got up and followed him to the door. 'D'you fancy a drink while you're here?'

Clarke drew open the door and shook his head gravely. 'Never touch the filthy stuff,' he grunted. 'I'll be seein' you around, eh?'

'Definitely.' Den watched the door swing shut and stood there gathering the fragments of his wits about him.

Angie came around the bar, absently gathering glasses. She stepped up close to Den, trying to figure out what had gone on. His face suggested he'd been hit over the skull with something heavy and blunt.

'More trouble?' she murmured.

Den turned to her. His smile spread suddenly and his eyes widened. 'No trouble at all, darlin'. I told you I could always handle things at the crunch, didn't I?'

'Yeah. You've told me a lot of things. So what's the score?'

'The fag business has been taken care of. Grazier's been taken care of. More than half our bleedin' worries have been taken care of.'

Angie glanced at the still-swinging door. 'Are you tellin' me you got that one to handle it for you?'

'Somethin' like that.' Impulsively Den grasped Angie's shoulders and kissed her forehead. 'What do you reckon to your old man now then, eh?'

'I reckon he's gettin' in with some bloody dodgy company.'

'Aw, don't be like that.' Den took the glasses from her and carried them to the bar. He put them down and turned to her, propping his elbows on the edge. 'Things are on the up. An' that's the way they'll keep goin' from now on.'

Angie still looked troubled. 'Den, people like that are the worst kind of news . . .'

'Not if they're handled right.' He winked. 'Feel better now about dinner on Saturday?'

She shrugged. 'I suppose I will, in a minute.'

Den faced the bar and spread his hands on the top. Angie had talked about a miracle earlier and bop! here was one, right in his lap. At a single stroke his peace of mind had been restored – or nearly – and his pride in himself was coming back at a gallop. It had worked, he thought. Face one problem and the others start to sort themselves out. He'd make that a policy and firm philosophy for life. Just for a fleeting second he thought of Jan and wished a repair job was possible there. But some losses, as he'd already told himself, had to be put up with. When Angie came alongside he turned and felt a tight, sudden pleasure at the sight of her.

'Everythin's goin' to be all right between us too, girl. You wait an' see.'

Angie nodded. She wanted, quite genuinely, to share his optimism. But that was still a fair way beyond her.

9

Jan had finished dictating into her pocket recorder and was in the kitchen making coffee when the street-level buzzer sounded. She went to the intercom and frowned at it. She could always pretend she was out, of course. But that was hardly her style. She left deviousness and deceit to her colleagues and anybody else who believed it got them anywhere. She touched the button and asked who was there.

'It's Irene,' a Mayfair-toned voice chirruped.

Jan sighed quietly. Maybe it would have been better to be devious, after all. 'Come on up,' she said brightly and pressed the switch to open the door.

When Irene came in she brought with her the whole negative aura of her type. She was thirty and tall, with expensively clipped dark hair and make-up that took more time to apply, Jan knew, than most responsible people could afford to waste in the morning. But then Irene was a woman of leisure, entirely without an occupation or ambition. She enjoyed simply being who she was.

'Darling.' Irene embraced Jan briefly then stepped back and unbuttoned her voluminous coat. Underneath she wore a yellow-gold shirt, beige jacket and mid-brown skirt that collectively would have cost, Jan guessed, approximately three days' profit at *The Queen Victoria*. In spite of herself, she continued to use that financial yardstick whenever she observed any lavishness she disapproved of.

'It's been ages, Irene.'

'Weeks,' Irene agreed, checking her face in the mirror across the room. It was a pouting, small-featured face, untouched by the marks of any worthwhile experience. 'I said to myself as I stepped out of the bath this morning, I simply must pop round and see Jan. Otherwise she'll think I'm snubbing her.'

'Oh, I wouldn't think that at all.' Jan waved Irene towards the kitchen. 'Come and have a coffee. It's nearly ready.' As they went into the kitchen and Irene eased herself delicately on to a stool, Jan reflected that even Saturdays weren't sacrosanct any more. There had been a time when she could have the entire weekend to herself had she felt like it, but the business of people making the social rounds had hotted up again recently. That was unfortunate, because she felt she had outgrown the Irenes of the world.

'So what have you been doing with yourself?'

Jan considered the question. It meant different things, depending on who asked it. In Irene's case, it meant what had she been doing outside of business hours and, for that matter, outside the boundaries of her normal social existence. Irene craved gossip; she would settle for the raw materials of gossip, though the steamier they were, the better.

'Nothing at all,' Jan said. She set out two cups and saucers. 'I've been too busy lately to do much more than get home, do the work I bring from the office with me, then collapse until morning.'

'Poor darling. How dull.'

As she poured the coffee Jan decided to head off

the inevitable fishing that would ensue, if she let it. 'Tell me about yourself,' she said. 'Been down to Esher lately?'

Irene seemed delighted to be asked. 'Oh yes, naturally. Only last weekend, as a matter of fact.' Her affair with young Captain Norton-Lindsay of the Grenadier Guards was a matter of great – though rather coy – pride to her. She wasn't in the least aware that most people thought Captain Norton-Lindsay was a twit and a crashing bore. 'We're having to be a teensy bit more careful lately, though. Eleanor's been acting all suspicious again.' Irene rolled her eyes elaborately as she accepted her coffee. 'Why she just can't give in gracefully I don't know.'

Jan smiled, though she felt more like laughing. Eleanor was the Captain's horse-faced fiancée; her grasp of sexual politics – like her understanding of most things – was sadly stunted. Jan suspected the girl probably couldn't sit the right way on a toilet. Eleanor had been left plenty of clues about the goings-on down in Esher – Irene had seen to that – and from time to time she created little scenes which added some excitement to Irene's little adventure.

'Do you think you'll marry the young man?' Jan tried to picture Irene married and trying to run a house. The impulse to laugh grew a shade stronger.

'One day, perhaps,' Irene said wistfully. 'Lord knows what Daddy would say, though. He's always hoped I'd settle down with somebody titled.'

'Well, there are certainly plenty of eligible, chinless hooray-Henries on the circuit,' Jan said, unable to resist the observation. 'But given your temperament, I suppose you prefer a man of action.'

Irene sipped her coffee daintily. 'Absolutely. Speaking of which – how's the little liaison going with your own man of action?'

Jan supposed there had been no way of avoiding the question, after all. 'I'm cooling it off, actually,' she said, knowing there was no point in lying. Word got around. It always did, whatever precautions were taken. 'Things haven't quite worked out.'

'Well.' Irene put on her candid face, which she did by bringing her eyebrows closer together. 'I have to say, darling, that I'm not the least bit surprised. He simply isn't you. I know we all like roughing it a bit from time to time, but that fellow . . .'

Jan glared at her. 'You're overstepping, Irene,' she warned sharply.

Irene was immediately contrite. 'Oh heavens, I didn't mean to hurt you, dearest. I was simply observing that it was – well, out of character for you to get involved with whatsisname.'

'Perhaps it was,' Jan said stiffly. Over the years she had taken pains to let no one on the circuit know just what *was* in character for her. She had always had a series of escorts, and still did, each one chosen as carefully as her clothes to suit a particular occasion. None of those men had ever been permitted to be intimate with her. They were components of a carefully developed social gloss. Lovers, the few she'd taken, had always been something else, a very private part of her life.

'I hope it hasn't been too traumatic for you,' Irene sighed, her voice rich with concern. 'I know how painful these little amputations can be.'

'Not too damaging, no . . .'

If only she hadn't been quite so public about her affair with Den, Jan thought, she wouldn't be exposed to all the little eddies of tittle-tattle and this hollow brand of sympathy. Not that she had really made it public. She had simply appeared in a couple of rather exclusive restaurants with him, and only once in each place, but even so they had been spotted by some society jackal or other; Den had been duly measured up, weighed, and found lacking. Perhaps she had wanted to be seen with him, though. She had certainly never felt ashamed of her attraction to him. If she admitted it, Den Watts had been the most special man in her life to date.

'Have you, um, found someone yet to fill the hollow, as it were?' Irene's eyes hardened a trace, watching for any evasion.

'It's rather early for that,' Jan said. 'And as I told you, I'm so busy these days, there's scarcely time for more than work and sleep.'

'I often wonder why you do work, darling. I mean it's not as if you have to, is it? You could be having a wonderful time, instead of knocking yourself out in that job of yours.'

'But I *am* having a wonderful time. I love my work, It's absorbing and it's challenging. Fulfilling, in fact. I can't see myself drawing any satisfaction from doing nothing but living off an inheritance, visiting people all the time, shopping, screwing at weekends for recreation and generally letting my brains and talent turn to silt.'

Irene was perfectly aware that her own empty life had just been described in one sentence. She drained

90

her cup and slipped elegantly off the stool. 'Look at the time,' she said. Her voice was rather too clipped.

'Going so soon?' Jan asked, feigning surprise. 'You've only just arrived.'

'I hadn't realized it was after eleven.' Irene flounced through to the sitting room with Jan behind her. 'There must be something up with my watch.' She snatched up her coat from the sofa and shrugged into it. 'I've lots to do before lunch . . .' She made a brittle smile and waved her hand at the papers scattered on the coffee table. 'Besides, I must leave you to get on with your work.'

At the door they embraced again briefly.

'I'll see you soon,' Jan said.

'Of course, darling. Look after yourself.' Opening the door, Irene couldn't resist firing a parting barb. 'Nice to know you're seeing things straight again, anyway.' Another crisp smile and she was gone.

Back in the kitchen Jan finished her coffee and washed the cups. She went back to the sitting room and picked up her little recorder. Irene's nasty remark about roughing it echoed in her mind. But stuff Irene, she thought. There were moments, moments like now, when she ached to see the man she had rejected, actually craved the feeling of him near her.

'You bastard, Den,' she said, but softly.

She had been careful never to analyse what made her feel about him the way she had; she'd warned Den himself never to try too hard to do that – 'If you want to dissect something,' she had said, 'first you have to kill it.'

Now she had killed it, anyway. There was an opportunity to dissect and analyse if she cared to. For a minute she tried, standing there alone in her large, quiet sitting room. No sure answer came. Perhaps he had been the other half of her. He could have been the rebellion she occasionally craved, the half-buried desire for a more basic existence – maybe he had answered the anger and frustration she sometimes felt against all the rules she obeyed so beautifully.

Now – well, he had hurt her terribly with his accusation and ugly mistrust. He had wounded her to the soul. The penalty she had exacted probably pained her as much as it had wounded him. But it was done, there was no undoing it. Jan was a businesswoman and she knew the value – indeed the necessity – to hold to her decisions, to make no policy U-turns. Without that kind of discipline life became messy, disordered and irksome. She had to be hard with herself as well as with him. It would all work out for the best.

'All for the best,' she whispered.

She looked around the room, feeling its emptiness, knowing he would never fill that space again with his laughter, his love.

'*Damn* you, Den Watts!'

Sudden, unreasonable tears overtook her as she drew back her arm and hurled the tape recorder at the wall.

10

The evening started well. Saturday-night crowds swelled the West End, generating an atmosphere of celebration, of people setting out in earnest pursuit of fun. Den and Angie got out of their cab at the corner of Tottenham Court Road and Oxford Street and walked arm in arm down through Soho and out across Regent Street, treading the routes of their courting days, confronting memories at every turn.

Den's choice of restaurant impressed Angie deeply. It was off Piccadilly, tucked away in a small street behind the Burlington Arcade. A liveried doorman gave Angie a curious look as she stepped past him, chains and bracelets rattling, resplendent in her striped fur, hip hugging black silk dress and shiny black-and-white stiletto-heeled shoes.

'Very up-market, Den,' she murmured as they were shown to a table in the corner. The carpet, snowy white, whispered under their feet and the legs of the chairs as they sat down. Angie looked around, taking in the opulent wall hangings, the tiny crystal chandeliers, the po-faced waiters and the people at other tables, wearing the unmistakable patina of wealth. Rich people always looked different, she had noticed. It even showed on their skin. She smiled back cheerfully as a few of them stared in her direction.

'Like it then, darlin'?' Den, in his newest C&A suit and lilac velvet bow tie, was beaming at her. 'I thought, what the hell, if it's gonna be special, let's make it *special*.'

'Oh, it's that, all right.'

'Fancy a drinkie for starters?' They had decided against visiting a wine bar first, reasoning that it would be better to spend a little longer in the restaurant.

'I'll say I do.' Angie considered what to have as a waiter came forward with the menus. 'What're you havin', Den?'

'A Tio Pepe, I think,' he said, addressing the waiter. 'Well chilled, of course.'

'Of course, sir,' the waiter mumbled stiffly. 'And madam?' He watched her with raised eyebrows, an expression that could be read several ways.

'Oh, I'll have a Bloody Mary, I think.'

The waiter nodded, his nostrils flaring slightly, and went away.

'Sniffy lookin' git, isn't he?' Angie observed.

'It's part of their trainin',' Den explained. 'They have to go round for six months with a rotten kipper tied under their hooters, just to get the expression right.'

Ordering presented a few problems. Den had been to the place only once before, with Jan. She had made the suggestions on that occasion and Den had completely forgotten, until now, that the entire menu was written in French.

'There's no prices in mine,' Angie said.

'There's stacks of them in mine,' Den grunted. 'It's the way they do things. The lady doesn't get to know it's costin' her escort an arm an' a leg.'

'So tell me what some of these things are.' Angie held the menu across to Den. 'What's that?' She

94

frowned at the page, trying to get her mouth round the words. 'Oofs en gel – oofs enn gelee? Is that how you say it? What's oofs?' She giggled, then sat back, startled as another waiter appeared at her shoulder.

'*Oeufs en gelee,*' he droned, in what sounded like immaculate French. 'It is two poached eggs, madam, served in aspic with slices of ham, flavoured with vermouth and garnished with dill and chervil.'

'Oh.' Angie made a face at Den. 'Don't think I like the sound of that.'

Den was raking his memory. 'Why don't you try the artichoke hearts, Angie? They serve them with an oil an' vinegar dressin'. Very tasty.'

She agreed to go for that and Den said he would have the same.

'*Artichaux aux vinaigrette,*' the waiter muttered, writing on his pad. 'And for the fish course – assuming sir and madam do not wish to go straight to the entree?'

Den's memory was coming back swiftly now. 'We'll skip the fish . . .' He glanced at Angie. 'It gets too fillin', otherwise,' he explained.

Patiently the waiter stood by as they struggled with their selection of main course dishes. Finally, after a couple of misunderstandings, Den ordered beef in red wine and Angie said she would have suprèmes of chicken in a white wine sauce.

As the waiter withdrew she leaned across the table, grinning. 'Imagine that – supreme's the French word for breast!'

Den looked around a little warily. People were listening. 'I think it's only when they're talkin' about chickens they call them that,' he muttered.

Angie chuckled and downed a third of her Bloody

Mary, which had arrived while they were ordering. 'You can imagine it, can't you? Some French bloke chattin' up an English bird – "My, what a pretty pair of supremes you 'ave zere, darleeng!"'

'Ange, cool it a bit.' Den glared over Angie's shoulder and stared down a dowager type who was directing her eyes, one along each side of her nose, at Angie's shoulder blades. 'Just keep it down an octave,' he said more softly. 'Sound carries dead easy in places like this.'

'Aw, don't be such a dry stick.' Angie drank some more and swirled the remains of the drink in front of her. 'We're here to enjoy ourselves, right? Don't go puttin' on the dampers before we've even started.'

'Don't worry, love.' Den forced a smile. 'I'll see you enjoy yourself.'

'Well . . .' Angie paused and drained the glass. She held it out to Den, smacking her lips. 'Maybe you can start by orderin' me another one of these. I don't know how they make them, but they're a bloody sight better'n the ones we make up.' She let out another giggle. 'I didn't mean it to come out like that – *bloody* sight, get it?'

'Yeah,' Den sighed, beckoning the waiter. 'I get it.' It was hard now to stifle his memories of this place. Last time the atmosphere at the table had been soft, warm and romantic. Tonight, he feared, it would be more like spending a night in a Munich bier keller.

His worst forebodings, as it turned out, had been well short of the mark. By the end of the main course Angie had consumed more than a bottle of Muscadet, while Den had only sipped at a half bottle of Beaujolais. One of them, he'd decided, had better stay in control. As the plates were cleared away Angie put her elbows on the table and looked at him dolefully.

'Do you really mean all this?' she asked him.

'All what?'

'This fresh start business.' Her tongue slurred the words, although her eyes were steady. 'Or are you just divertin' my attention from somethin'?'

'Such as what?'

'Such as your bird.'

Den looked about him again, then leaned close to Angie. 'What're you on about?'

'I know about her, Den. I've known a long time.'

Unable to meet her eyes, he stared at the bridge of her nose. 'Rubbish. I'm tryin' to make this the beginnin' of a new era for us, just like I said. Now forget all that twaddle about another woman. There isn't one.'

'She uses nice blue notepaper,' Angie drawled.

Den had wondered about that note. He'd known he had it on him and had meant to destroy it, but when he went through his pockets it had gone. After a while he stopped wondering about it. Now he was being told, in a not-too roundabout way, that Angie was holding it as evidence. After some swift thinking, he decided to short-circuit the lies and counter-assertions.

'Angie,' he said huskily, reaching for her hand. 'This is the *new* start, I swear to you. Nothing that's past matters.' He watched her eyes soften. *Thank God for that*, he thought.

'All right,' she said. 'I believe you, darlin',' She returned the pressure of his fingers. 'Let's celebrate it with a drop of champagne, eh?'

'Are you sure?' He tried not to look too anxious. 'I mean, you haven't had your sweet yet.'

'I'm full up, I don't want any.' She squeezed his fingers again. 'Go on, order up a bottle. Let's get into the new life in style.'

The champagne lasted less than half an hour; it would have been finished much sooner if Angie hadn't kept proposing little toasts between gulps. Den felt his head getting light and wondered what must be happening to hers. From the look of her, she was no longer receiving light or sound in straight lines.

Suddenly, on the dregs of the last glass, Angie shot to her feet, swerved round and addressed the entire restaurant. 'Everybody join us in a toast, eh?' she yelled, raising her glass and slopping the drink on her knuckles. 'To our new life! Fresh horizons an' all that!'

The head waiter came across, looking grave. 'Madam, I must ask you to resume your seat.'

Angie stared at him, swaying gently. 'Resume it? How do I do that?'

'Please sit down, Madam. You are disturbing the other customers.'

'No I'm not.' She smiled past the man's shoulder, impervious to the stony faces glaring back at her. 'They're joining us in a toast.' She hiccupped softly. 'They are, aren't they, Den? Get them some bubbly, waiter, so they can get in on the action.'

As she turned to grin at the other diners again her elbow caught a jardiniere of flowers on the ledge by the table and sent it crashing to the floor. 'Oh, God, I'm sorry,' she whined. She bent to help pick up the pieces. Gravity took advantage of her impaired balance and she performed an involuntary, sideways somersault into the wreckage, She landed with her knees in the air, leaving no doubt as to the colour and quality of her underwear.

For Den the next five minutes, added to the previous fifteen, assumed the proportions of a nightmare. Between picking up Angie, silencing her, brushing her down, silencing her again, paying the bill and negotiating the distance from the table to the door, he became so enmeshed in confusion and embarrassment that he forgot to leave a tip. At the door the head waiter stiffly informed him that neither he nor his wife would be welcome there ever again. Angie, in parting, told the man he could stick his restaurant where the monkey stuck its nuts.

Somehow they got back to Walford. The pub was closed and in darkness. Den had to prop Angie against the wall while he fumbled out his keys and opened the door. When they were finally inside Angie staggered behind the bar, put on the lights and announced she wanted another drink.

Now that his head was clearing and the last waves of embarrassment were ebbing, Den began to feel anger. He stood by the door, glaring at her. 'Don't you think you've had enough, you booze-soaked slut?'

'Don't be like that, Den,' she pouted, entering the mushy phase of her condition. 'I need a drinkie to help me sleep.' She stumbled forward and leaned on the bar. 'Unless you've got other ideas, of course.' She winked. 'Know what I mean?'

He knew what she meant and the idea of it made him cringe. 'Don't be ridiculous, Ange. I want you to get up them stairs, now, an' get yourself into bed. Don't bother tryin' to undress, you'd only strangle yourself. Just flop into it an' get some kip.'

'Aw, Den . . .' She made to come round the bar, took two steps and landed on her knees with a bang. 'Ow! God! I've busted me kneecaps!'

Den didn't feel inclined to help her up. He waited until her head appeared above the edge of the bar, then told her, again, to get to bed.

'Don't think I can make it on me own,' she said helplessly. 'Give us a hand, eh?'

With a lot of bumping, shoving and pulling, he finally got her to the top of the stairs and opened her bedroom door. 'In you go,' he ordered. 'An' try to be quiet about it. Sharon's asleep.'

Angie gripped his arm suddenly. 'Come on,' she breathed against his ear. 'Come with me.'

'Leave off, Ange. I'm goin' to me own room.'

'But you promised.'

'I did not,' he said indignantly.

Angie peered at him, her eyes all dewy-soft. 'New start, you said. Isn't comin' to bed with me part of the new start?' She snuffled against his shoulder for a moment. 'What kind of fresh beginnin' is it with you stickin' to your own room like a big frightened kid?'

That stung him, even allowing for the fact that she was drunk. Any suggestion that he was frightened of sex had always cut him deeply. That was largely because, in his younger days, the mechanics and responsibilities of two-person sex had daunted him terribly. Angie had helped him over that, only to undermine him again when they were married.

'Den?' She looked up into his face. 'Just come an' cuddle me for a bit, eh? It's all I'm askin', for now.'

Perhaps because he was tired, or because the prospect of missing Jan yet another night was too much to face, he sighed and eased her ahead of him into the room.

'No need to put on the light, Ange. Just get in, I'll get undressed over here.'

He moved to the shadowy side of the room, away from the dim glow of the street lamps. In the darkness he could hear her moving softly, grunting every few seconds, then he heard the bedsprings creak. Cautiously, in his underpants and singlet, he crept to the bed and slipped in beside her.

'Cuddle up,' Angie moaned, her voice muffled by the covers.

Den slid nearer, his arm curved. He closed it over her as his body meshed to the curl of her back. He nuzzled the pillows, relishing the softness, then he realized something. She was naked. As he began to back slowly away Angie turned to face him, her arms reaching out.

'Den, Den,' she groaned. Her knees brushed his, then her legs straightened suddenly and she was pressing her body at him, warming him with her skin. 'Den, darlin' . . .'

He rolled sideways sharply and in one move he was on his feet by the bed. He heard her push herself up on an elbow.

'What the hell's up?' she demanded.

'Nothin's up,' he snapped. 'Just get to sleep, eh? You're workin' in the bar in the mornin', remember.'

He gathered his clothes, stamped across the room and heard her call him a useless bastard an instant before he closed the door behind him.

In his own room he got into his pyjamas and dived under the covers, shivering against the cold sheets. As the warmth began to gather, so did the misery, his old nightly companion. Jan was gone but he couldn't stop missing her. Even though he always slept alone at The Vic, her love had been a cushion against his disheartening, arrid domestic life. Without even the solace of that, he felt desolate.

So much for fresh beginnings, he thought. The grand equation – ATTACK ONE PROBLEM, THE OTHERS SORT THEMSELVES OUT – seemed very suspect now. More likely that it should run ATTACK SOME PROBLEMS AND YOU'LL NEVER WIN: OTHERS SOMETIMES GET SORTED OUT BY LUCK.

He slid towards sleep trying to keep a mental fix on such gains as he had made. He was out of trouble with the law, for the time being. He was in the good books of a man who would make a very handy ally, should he ever need one.

That was all, though. And it was nothing. When sleep finally closed in he knew it with a cold, glum certainty. No gains, no advances. This was square one, the world as it had been before. Life went on keeping him at a distance from real happiness. And he was married to a woman dedicated to much the same thing.

11

During the month that followed, The Vic's up-front policy of service with nothing but a smile showed signs of strain. In the mornings Angie still showed the customers a cheerful front, but there was no doubt she became rather curt towards one o'clock. By afternoon closing time she was definitely edgy, like someone trying to be sociable in a pair of tight shoes. Come evening, she barely managed to be civil.

Den wasn't his usual glib self, either. He was by turns distant, stiff, irritable, just occasionally jocular – and then only when he was forced to react to someone else's sense of humour. He would listen to a joke and laugh at it, but there was nothing spontaneous in the sound he made; it was a false, almost guttural response that left him as fast as it came, with no after-smile, no light of amusement in his eyes. He was noticeably cold towards Angie and openly hostile to people he didn't like. He appeared to have abandoned his showmanship and most of his old personality. In its place there was just a moody, often irascible character who seemed to have a hard time just getting through the day.

'I reckon he's goin' right off,' Nick Cotton remarked to his mother as they watched Den from a corner of the bar one lunchtime. 'I can tell when a bloke's got somethin' turnin' bad in him. Mark my word, old Den's goin' down the chute.'

Dot Cotton waggled her head in agreement. Anything her Nick said was probably right. Dot was a tall, lean, nervously disordered woman, with eyes that looked permanently startled and a mouth built for disapproval. Ever since her husband had run out on her, years before, she had turned to Nick for moral support, for reassurance, plus the solace she needed so badly when one or other of her neurotic complaints attacked her.

'It's the greed in that one's soul that's the trouble,' she murmured, toying with her orange juice.

Nick squinted at her, pursing his mean little mouth. 'What's greed got to do with it?' Greed, as it happened, was one of Nick's principal blemishes, running a close second to his crookedness. 'I was talkin' about somethin' eatin' away at Den, not somethin' he's sick to lay his hands on.'

'Greed eats at a man. He's got it in him like a cancer.' Dot's head waggled again as she puffed on her cigarette. 'There's greed in his eyes when he looks at a woman, any woman. It's there when he counts money an' all.' She cleared her throat, preparing for a quote. 'Hell and destruction are never full, so the eyes of man are never satisfied. The Book of Proverbs.'

Nick thought about that, but only for a couple of seconds. 'Buy us a pint, will you Mum?'

'I bought you that one.'

'Yeah, but I'm a bit short.' He saw another Bible quotation coming and added hastily, 'If you can't afford it, never mind. I'll go without.' He knew that any show of self-denial on his part always made his mother relent, and it got her off the religious hobby horse.

'Oh, I daresay I can stretch to another drink for you.' She got out her purse.

'Ta, Mum. You're a gem.' Nick rapped the bottom of his glass sharply on the bar.

'Yeah?' Den turned and stared at him.

'Pint, please.'

With slow, measured tread Den came along the bar and stopped opposite Nick. 'I've got eyes in me head,' he said, barely moving his lips. 'I scan this bar regularly, minute by minute. I'd soon have noticed you were wantin' a drink.'

Nick frowned at him, nervously fingering his earring. 'So what?'

'So don't bang the bleedin' glass on the bar top. All right?'

Nick chewed his lip, wishing this was a smaller, much more timid man he was confronting. 'Yeah,' he said at last. 'Got it.'

'Fine.' Den snatched the glass and walked back to the pump. He pulled a pint of bitter, taking much more time than was necessary, then walked slowly back to Nick and put down the drink. 'Sixty pence.'

'Mum's payin',' Nick mumbled, picking up the drink.

'What a surprise.' Den switched his jaundiced gaze to Dot. 'What it is to have a son that looks after you, eh?'

'I've no complaints,' Dot snapped.

Den picked up the handful of mixed coins she had scraped from her purse. 'Yes, it must be a grand thing to know you've got a man about the place who'll see you right, come what may.' He shot Nick a frigid smile. 'Where are you workin' these days?'

'I've a couple of offers I'm considerin'.' To Nick,

who was used to doing the leaning, this was a particularly uncomfortable exchange. He sipped his pint, hoping Den would go away.

'He's got very good prospects,' Dot cut in defensively. 'He just has to be choosy, that's all. It'd be silly to take second best. With the references he's got, he could get a good job anywhere.'

'References? Him?'

'That's what I said.'

'You mean from his metal-work instructor at Borstal? Or the head screw at the Scrubs – that kind of thing?'

Nick usually moved in small, calculated stages, as if there were cameras filming him, but he lost his self-awareness suddenly and leaned swiftly across the bar. 'Listen you, I don't have to take that kind of thing. I'm a member of the public, right? I expect a bit of civility off a barman.'

Den's hand shot out and caught one leather lapel, twisting it. 'What you'll get off this one is a thick lip if you don't watch it! An' I ain't a barman, get that into your loaf. I'm the tenant of this public house.' He released Nick's collar but went on glaring at him. 'I make the rules in here. One of them is, there's to be no foulin' of the bar stools.'

Nick blinked. 'I never fouled your bloody stool.'

'No? You're sittin' on it, aren't you?'

'Come on Nick,' Dot wailed, rising and grasping her son's arm. 'We didn't come in here to have you insulted.'

Den folded his arms. 'Where do you usually go, then?'

Nick gulped down the pint with his mother tugging

106

at his arm. As he put the empty glass on the bar he gave Den the hard, dangerous look he normally used for purposes of coercion, extortion or blackmail. 'You'll get yours, Watts,' he growled.

'Yeah, sure I will,' Den sighed. 'Look at the state I'm in, just thinkin' about it. Thank God I put on me brown trousers.'

Nick allowed his mother to drag him out. Den stood where he was, watching the door.

'Pleased with yourself, big man?'

He didn't turn, but he could feel Angie's presence behind him like a poised pitchfork.

'Good bit of sport, was it, pickin' on poor old Dot an' pint-size Nick? I never see you takin' on any real challenges around here. Dockers an' such can spit on the floor, eff an' blind for all they're worth an' all you do is smile an' call them mate.' Angie jabbed his shoulder. 'I'm talkin' to you!'

'Poke me like that one more time,' Den said quietly, still with his back to her, 'An' I'll make you eat the bloody finger.'

She scowled at the back of his jacket. 'Some chance you'd have, Super-Guy. I'd only have to threaten you with sex an' you'd be off like a budgie with a cat behind it.'

Den turned, ready to let her have both barrels, but she was already along the bar, rendering service with a tight smile. He went through to the back, opened the cellar door and climbed down into the draughty chamber that had become, increasingly, his retreat.

He sat down on an upturned crate and rested his chin on his hands. He was always safe from the world down here, he thought, staring along the rows of barrels with their snaking plastic pipes. Safe from the wife, anyway, whose malice and eternally nerve-wracking presence made up so much of his dismal world. Angie would never come down here. She was terrified of spiders, and fortunately the place was crawling with them.

In the almost-four weeks since the disastrous Ceremony of the Fresh Start, Den had sunk steadily into a condition of spiritual greyness, an interior gloom that was hardly new to him, but which now appeared to have set in permanently. Before, he had always pulled himself out of the depths of boredom, or self-pity, or whatever else made him feel low. It was automatic, he'd never had to wait long for the will and the power to do it. This time, the cold war upstairs had managed to keep him flat on his emotional face and remove any strength on his part to get up and start boxing again.

'Sod the bloody lot of it,' he muttered to a half-empty barrel of Luxford and Copley's bitter. A whole, long, psychiatric history could be put together about the criss-crossing strands of aggro and alienation that made up his existence with Angie, but it could all be said quite simply. Angie needed sex and respect from him. She didn't get either. He needed Jan and all she still meant to him, plus some esteem from his wife. He was without both. End of case diagnosis. Patients unlikely to be cured.

He couldn't remember how many times he had tried to speak to Jan since the cock-up 'phone call. The last time had been over a week ago. He had tried to tell her that, try as he might, he couldn't get over her. He still loved her as much as ever. As usual, Jan put down the 'phone before he could get under way.

Den knew, of course, that because he had failed to improve things at home, his isolation – therefore his intensified need for Jan – had become unbearable. Except that he *did* bear it and took out his frequent anguish on everything and everybody.

Some days he was blinded to everything but the image of Jan, as if it were branded on the tissue of his brain. Loyalty to that image might have faltered, or diminished, if his effort at making it up with Angie hadn't gone so farcically wrong. As it was, he couldn't even fake some desire for his wife, not with Jan taking up so much of his need. And without a sign of him needing her, Angie couldn't feel the respect he needed so badly from *her*. It was some state of affairs.

He smiled wryly, remembering a desperate scheme he'd hatched a couple of weeks before. If he got himself drunk enough, he had reasoned, he could force his randiness to overcome his scruples. Then he could haul Angie off to bed.

Fired by the idea, he had tanked himself up steadily throughout one Friday evening, all the time reminding himself of his wife's considerable physical allure and her talent between the sheets. By closing time he was in a perfect frame of mind to ravish Angie. She was cool at his first approach, but gradually she warmed to the idea of ending hostilities and getting into bed. They closed up the pub quickly and retired.

The outcome had been more farce, more misery and an escalation of the cold war. Den had been in the right frame of mind all right, but he wasn't in the necessary frame of body. The droop persisted in spite of every effort Angie made. Den finally crept away, scorned and rejected. In his own room he slept fitfully, haunted by erotic dreams of Jan.

'You skulkin' down there again?' Angie's voice rattled round the walls, startling Den and making the spiders wary.

He groaned. 'Yeah, I'm here. What is it?'

'There's a man to see you.'

'Can't you attend to him? I'm havin' trouble with one of the feed lines.'

'He's been sent by the brewery. They told him to speak to the gaffer. That's you, remember?' Her voice took on extra harshness as she added, 'The big macho number with his name above the door.'

When he reached the bar Den found a man of about forty, smart-suited, with a handsome, amiable face and a handshake that was firm and confident.

'Nice to meet you, Mr Watts. I'm John Fairchild.'

'How d'you do.' Den tried to look cordial. 'You're from the brewery, I hear.'

'No. I'm a sales representative with Milton Autovend.'

Den dropped the cordiality. 'I don't want anythin', Mr Fairchild. Sorry your journey's been wasted.' He turned away.

'Ah – Mr Larkin said you'd be pleased to talk over the proposition I've brought along.'

The name of the Area Manager put the brake on Den. He turned back to the salesman. 'How come he said that?'

'The brewery is interested in backing any tenant who installs our new equipment,' Fairchild explained pleasantly. 'They'll meet the cost of installation, which is very generous of them, I'd say. That way, your profits begin from day one of operation.'

Den had heard patter of that sort lots of times, but never in connection with brewery approval. The conclusion to be drawn was ominously clear. If Den went for the equipment the brewery would approve, if he didn't then they'd disapprove. He couldn't afford even a scrap of displeasure from that quarter.

'Let's go an' sit down, Mr Fairchild.'

The deal took ten minutes to discuss and conclude. The vending point – a small machine for the sale of coffee and tea – would be installed entirely at the brewery's expense. Stocking the machine with essences, milk, sugar and paper cups would be down to Den, and he would be required to purchase a minimum thirty-pounds' worth of supplies a week.

In Den's own idea it was a crazy idea. He would lose out. In no time at all his cellar would be crammed with redundant packets of tea and coffee and all the other junk. His punters didn't come into a pub to have tea parties or coffee mornings. They were boozers who came in to get stunned, not stimulated. But the brewery was all for enhancing its image; it would have pubs that catered to everybody, even teetotallers. So there was no wisdom in arguing, not if Den wanted to avoid making waves. He agreed to sign on the line and swallow the loss some way or another.

'Let me buy you and your wife a drink before I go,' Fairchild suggested as he tucked the completed papers into his briefcase.

'Very kind of you.' Den didn't feel like a drink, but vindictiveness had to have its way, whenever possible.

He stepped up to the bar with Fairchild beside him. 'Angie, you got a minute?'

She finished serving a customer and turned to them, managing in her unique way to freeze Den and show the salesman some warmth at the same time.

'This gentleman would like to buy us both a drink.'

'Oh.' Angie fluttered her eyelashes. 'That's really nice of you, erm – you did say your name's Mr Fairchild, didn't you?'

'That's right. But please, call me John.'

'Well, many thanks, John.' She made another flutter. 'I'll have a gin and tonic, if it's all the same to you.' She paused suddenly and frowned, staring intently at the salesman. 'Oh, now I've got it,' she said, brightening. 'Did anybody ever tell you, you're a dead ringer for that other John. You know, the one on the box, John Thaw? You're a lot younger, of course.'

Here we go again, Den thought. At every turn, at any opportunity at all, she did it on him. 'Mine's a brandy, thanks,' he grunted. 'Make it a big one.'

Late that night, when the pub was closed and Angie had gone to her bedroom, Den sat alone in the kitchen with a half bottle of scotch for company. The alcohol didn't make him feel any better, it simply helped him to feel less bad. He sat drinking steadily and wondered if it would always be like this. There were no signs of a change on the horizon, after all. He had often seen old defeated landlords in rundown pubs, men whose first stop in the morning was at one of the optics, men who drank all day as a substitute for their lost ability to hope. He could see himself ending up like that.

As Den grew slightly more depressed at the prospect,

a dim, familiar light flared at the back of his mind. He contemplated it, as he had done night after night lately. Usually it faded quickly. Tonight, maybe because he had drunk more than usual, it didn't seem quite so ready to turn dark.

'Try, try, try again,' he murmured.

It was the one direction in which he still felt inclined to make an effort. The light was his solitary, illogically stubborn beacon of hope.

He crept downstairs and picked up the telephone. Cautiously and slowly he began to dial. On the second last digit his heart nearly leapt out of his chest as Angie's voice tore the air.

'Late-night love call, is it?' she demanded from the top of the stairs.

Den dropped the receiver. He glared up at her. 'What's it to you?'

'Nothin' at all, lover. You'll do what you're doin' anyway, there's no point in me tryin' to stop you.' She came halfway down the stairs, pulling her dressing gown about her. 'I'd just like you to know somethin'. There's affairs an' affairs. You no doubt think you're entitled to yours – '

'I am *not* havin' an affair!'

'Maybe you're not,' she said blithely. 'Maybe you're just tryin' at present, though God knows who'd want you.'

'Get to bed, Ange. Right now.'

'I said I'd like you to know somethin', dearest.' She leaned forward from the waist, gripping the handrail. 'I'm as entitled to a bit of diversion as you are. Maybe I'm more entitled. So I'm servin' you notice. This girl's goin' to show you what havin' an affair's all about. I

113

won't say when it'll happen, but just you believe me, it's goin' to.' She turned and strode back up to her room.

Den turned and looked at the telephone. He reached out to it, then let his hand drop away again. The little beacon, he realized, had gone completely dark.

12

Two weeks before Christmas Ali Osman approached Den outside the launderette on Bridge Street.

'Fancy a game this Saturday night, do you? It's about time you chanced your arm again.'

Den was carrying a pile of freshly laundered bar towels with his chin resting on the bundle to steady it. He made a sour face at Ali. 'I suppose you're hopin' to get some Christmas spendin' money out of me.'

'Don't be daft. I'm offerin' you an opportunity to get your own back.'

'What – is it the same crowd as before, then?'

'Yeah.'

Den thought for a moment then shook his head, almost overbalancing the towels. 'The way my luck's runnin' just lately, I'd get cleaned out again. I can't afford to risk it.'

Ali looked surprised. 'That ain't like you, Den. You've always been one for takin' risks. You even told me life wasn't much without a regular risk or two, remember?'

'Yeah, I know that, but – '

'You *like* gamblin'.'

Den considered his position again. It was true, he loved playing poker, especially with the kind of stakes that set him at terrible risk. The very mention of a game put a jump of anticipation across his heart. Except for now; Ali's suggestion hadn't thrilled him in the least. Along with all his other enthusiasms, he seemed to have lost his love of a game of chance. That was a bad sign, as bad as any. Maybe he should make an effort to do something about it.

'Yeah, I have to admit, I've a strong gambler's streak.'

'Are you on, then?'

'Dunno. Speak to me later. Come in an' have a drink in about quarter of an hour, if you can manage it.'

Ali groaned. 'I never get a direct yes or no out of you, do I?'

'No, you don't,' Den agreed. 'Mind you, that was a direct answer, wasn't it?' He moved off, leaving Ali muttering.

The pub was busy. As Den came in, the trader from the market cheese stall was taking a tray with six pints on it to a table by the door. At the bar about a dozen men were jostling to get served as Angie shuttled back and forth pulling pints, taking money, handing out change and keeping up a steady stream of banter, directed at whoever was nearest. She glanced sharply at Den as he brought the towels behind the bar.

'Give us a hand here, for God's sake,' she yelled. 'I'm run off me feet.'

Den dumped the towels on a crisp box and took off his jacket. 'Right, who's first for servin'?' He rolled up his sleeves as three people answered him at once. 'Can you sort it out amongst yourselves an' let me know?'

The crowd was dealt with rapidly and when most of them had dispersed Angie told Den she had to go out for a few minutes.

'I shan't be long. There's just a couple of things I need off the market.'

'Carry on, Duchess. I'll keep an eye on the peasants an' make sure they don't get out of hand.'

As Den watched her put on her coat and hurry out, he reflected on the change in her during the past week. From a sullen, snarling, reluctant helpmate she had become almost the old Angie again. She was buoyant and energetic, she kept her jibes to a minimum and there had been no more talk about a revenge affair. Although they were still far from being friends, it seemed Angie was determined to keep as much harmony about the place as the circumstances would allow. Den wondered if she was starting to accept things again, instead of spending her days in all-out conflict with her situation. Whatever the reason for the change, life around The Vic was a lot less tense and Den was grateful enough for that.

Outside it was so cold that there was nothing unusual in the sight of someone hurrying along the pavement. Even so, Angie's speed was enough to raise the curiosity of Lou Beale and Ethel Skinner as she hurtled past them in the square. They watched her for a moment, then looked at each other and shrugged.

At the corner by Dr Legg's surgery Angie did a swift right turn. She was going so fast she almost collided with the telephone box. Breathless, she pulled open the door and slipped inside. She stood panting for a minute before she rested a coin on the slot and dialled.

John Fairchild answered at once.

'God, I'm sorry, love,' Angie said, still short of breath. 'We were that busy I couldn't ring you any earlier. Has it made you late for anythin', havin' to wait like that?'

He assured it hadn't. There was a lot of work to do in the office anyway and he'd been catching up on it when she called.

'Good. I can't hang on long now anyway, so you can get right back to what you're doin'.'

He asked her if it was all right for Saturday.

'Absolutely. I've arranged with my friend Kathy to stand in for me – I've told Den I'm goin' to see an old friend, a landlady who's been poorly on an' off for months. He didn't bat an eyelid.'

John Fairchild said he was glad she could make it. He had arranged a little surprise.

'Great. I love surprises. The nice kind anyway. What'll we say, about half-seven, eh? Corner of Botham Street and Carver Road?'

He promised he would pick her up at that place and time.

'Smashin'. I'll see you Saturday, then.' She made a kissing sound at the mouthpiece. 'Can hardly wait.'

As she came out of the box she took a deep, satisfied breath and began strolling back to the pub. Twists of fate, she was thinking, were among the most fascinating things in life. If she had managed to line up something with Jimmy Solomon, this probably wouldn't have happened. Set alongside John Fairchild, Jimmy was definitely the lesser bargain. John was sophisticated, charming and considerate. He was also a man who'd had a lot of experience with women, and that was a sizeable bonus.

It had been so easy to set up, too. The day he came to The Vic to supervise the installation of the vending machine, Angie had played up to him. It turned out he was interested anyway, and he had admitted later that he would have made a play for her even if she hadn't been so willing. Within ten days of their first meeting, they were lovers. Until now, they had been seeing each other on her nights off. Angie still had difficulty believing her luck. The biggest difficulty of all, though, was keeping herself from looking too cheerful around the pub.

By the fruit and vegetable stall she stopped and took Kathy Beale aside.

'It's all fixed for Saturday, love. You can still stand in, can't you?'

Kathy nodded. 'I'll be there, an' before you ask, I'll be able to cope.' She glanced sidelong at Pete. He was occupied with a customer. 'Are you sure *you* can?'

'Can what?'

'Cope. With what you're gettin' up to.'

'Course I can,' Angie said. 'Listen Kath, this has done me more good than two psychiatrists an' a month on a health farm. Don't worry about me.'

'I'll try not to.'

In the bar Den was serving a customer and trying to talk to Ali Osman at the same time. Ali gave Angie a wary smile as she came in.

'I'll see you then,' he said to Den. 'An' remember, just think lucky.' He emptied his glass and went out.

Angie took off her coat and joined Den behind the bar.

'About Saturday night,' he said, then broke off to serve Arthur Fowler, who had dropped in for a quick one in his lunch break.

Angie stared at him, feeling a little flurry of panic in

119

her breast. She was still staring when he finished serving Arthur and came back.

'What about Saturday?'

'Can you put off visitin' Maisie?' Den asked her. 'I've arranged to get into a card game.'

Angie stiffened. 'I made my arrangements first.'

'I know that. But you can see Maisie any old time, can't you? There's not many opportunities for a good game of cards these days.'

'But I promised her I'd be round.'

Den sighed and gazed at the floor for a moment. 'Ange. How often do I get out? Eh? What opportunities do I have for doin' much else but work behind this bleedin' bar all the time?'

Anxiety was making her think fast. 'Look, you've as many opportunities as I've got, you just don't take them. I've promised a sick friend I'm goin' to visit her an' that's that. I keep my promises.'

'An' I keep mine,' Den countered. 'I've just promised I'll make up a five-hander, an' nothin' nor nobody's goin' to stop me.'

Angie made an effort to keep the panic out of her voice. 'We'll just have to get the part-time barman in, then.'

'He's left,' Den pointed out. 'You know he has.'

'Then poach one!'

Den suddenly looked puzzled. 'Look, what's the problem here? You've said before that visitin' sick people bores the backside off you. I'd have thought you'd get a lot more kicks stoppin' here an' chattin' up the punters without me to hinder you.'

She stifled an impulse to tell him she wouldn't

let him hinder her anyway. 'It's like I said, Den, I *promised*.'

'Bloody hell,' he grunted. 'You're gettin' to be a regular concerned citizen, aren't you?' He studied the determination on her face for a moment, then sighed. 'OK, I'll find us a barman from somewhere. But I'm not doin' this again, mind.'

'You won't have to, if you make your plans well ahead of time.'

As she stomped off through to the back Angie couldn't resist a private grin of relief. She never did like things going too easily anyway, she thought. So far her affair with John Fairchild had been a pure doddle. It had been time to hit a sticky patch, just for luck.

Dr Legg sat back and smiled reassuringly at his young visitor. 'I can understand how you feel, Sharon. But I can also see you're letting this difficulty expand in your head – do you understand what I mean? There's a problem, but it's not quite so big as you're making it.'

'That's what Michelle's always tellin' me,' she said sullenly.

'And Michelle's right.' Legg stroked one bushy eyebrow absently. 'A lot of the trouble nowadays is that young people are told how badly they should feel about their parents' disagreements. Television and magazines are forever preaching about how difficult it is for youngsters to *adjust* to upheavals in the home. I'm sure someone your age must feel practically obliged to turn insecure.'

'But it does upset me, Doctor,' Sharon insisted. 'I mean it's like being lost sometimes – you know, not knowing where to turn, what to do, how to get your bearings.'

Harold Legg was pretty sure she'd read that somewhere. Nevertheless, the girl did need some heartening advice. She wouldn't have come to him if the matter had been entirely trivial.

'Tell me this, Sharon. Do you think the strife between your mother and father can be cured?'

She shook her head. 'It's a habit with them. It just gets worse.'

'Are things bad all the time, or are there good spells?'

She shrugged. 'Just now things are all right, more or less. At least they're not arguin', or shoutin'. They're mostly ignorin' each other.'

'Yet you picked now to come and see me.'

Sharon nodded. 'I was hopin' you could tell me somethin' that'd make it easier to live with when they started up again.'

Harold smiled. 'You're an astute young lady, aren't you?' He leaned forward and folded his hands on the desk. 'Listen, then. If you think things'll get no better between your folks, what you have to do is find the strength to put yourself at a safe distance from what's hurting you.'

She frowned at him. 'Sorry, I don't think I understand that.'

'Maybe I can explain it better by telling you about myself. Did you know I was once married?'

'Yes. Your wife was killed during the war, wasn't she? Michelle's Gran told me.'

Harold was nodding. 'My wife was called Judith. She died not fifty yards from here, in the back garden of the house above this surgery.' He shook his head, remembering. 'When she died, Sharon, I was nearly insane with grief. For weeks I shut myself up in the house and let the pain devour me, inch by inch.'

Sharon bit her lip. 'It must have been awful.' She had often imagined how she would feel if she lost anyone close to her. The trouble was, she couldn't imagine feeling grief for either Den or Angie, even though she knew she would be bound to. 'But you got over it, didn't you?'

'That's the point I'm coming to,' Harold said. 'I almost packed in medicine – I nearly packed in living, come to that. I just wanted to fade away, and as fast as possible. Then something happened. At the time I thought it was automatic, but the more I've thought of it over the years, the more I've come to realize that it was something I consciously did for myself.'

'What?'

'I rediscovered my human dignity – my responsibility to myself, the need to give my own life a chance to develop and happen. The grief I suffered was caused by something outside of my personality, Sharon, it came from another part of me. I had to shield myself from that onslaught.'

Sharon was concentrating, trying to take it in. 'What was it you did, exactly?'

'I made myself behave as if nothing had happened. I cleaned up my house, I did repairs, tidied myself up and forced myself to see my friends again. All the while the grief was still attacking me, but I was wearing a tin hat on my emotions, if you like – I wasn't so vulnerable to it any more.'

'That's a bit like singing when you're scared of the dark.'

'Precisely. A day came when I could think of that awful loss, open my whole mind to it, and lo and behold, it didn't torture me any more. The grief had petered out because it got no encouragement. All I felt, in the end, was a kind of sweet sadness. I could live with what happened, because I had taken the torturing part out of it. From that moment on, everything improved.'

'But you still miss her, don't you?'

He smiled. 'Yes, I do. Every day of my life. But the loss hasn't crippled me – if anything, it's made me a stronger person than I might have been.'

There was a long silence between them, Harold watching Sharon as she studied her clasped fingers and thought over what he had told her.

'Do you see what I'm getting at?' he asked her finally.

'I think I do, sort of . . .'

'You have to believe in your own dignity as a human being, that's the first step. You're entitled to grow and develop as a person. Don't let anything harm that growth. Your parents' problems aren't yours, Sharon.'

'I've got to hear them, though.'

'Make yourself believe you're independent of it all. Pay more attention to improving your own life and try as hard as you can to ignore the squabbling and the tension. Don't moan about it to your friends – talk to them about other things, get involved with them as much as you can. You'll be amazed how well it works.'

Sharon sighed. 'I'm not so sure it's that easy . . .'

'It's not easy at all. But it's a lot better than letting

124

things wear you down.' He gave her his broadest smile. 'You're a bright girl, Sharon, and you've the strength of mind to put yourself above the troubles at home. Take your doctor's word for it.'

When Sharon left the surgery she looked a lot brighter than when she had come in. Dr Legg sat thinking about her for a few minutes. He knew that what he had told her was only part practical advice; the rest was tranquillizer – a compound of mild flattery and moderate exaggeration. It wasn't easy for a child to blossom without the encouragement and example of the parents. But it wasn't impossible either. She might just make it.

As he put away her case card he reflected that, when Sharon finally hit puberty, the problem of insecurity would perhaps come back – if it ever went away at all. He would try to tackle that when it happened, and in the meantime he'd hope it never would.

As for Den and Angie, Dr Legg's talent for personality diagnosis led him to believe they would never improve. He also suspected that, just like germs and living tissue, they couldn't survive without each other.

13

Like someone trying to catch a festive spirit and finding
he's the only one who can't, Den looked round the
dingy little office in Robbie Wood's shop and wondered
why he'd said he would come. The enthusiasm and the
necessary excitement weren't in him, although the
others were obviously keyed up and ready for action.

'One more little drink,' Robbie wheezed, unscrewing
the bottle cap, 'and we'll get down to it.'

'Just a small one for me,' Wally Simpson murmured.
He was standing by the table, drumming his fingers
softly on the top. Last time, Den hadn't noticed the
nervousness of the man. He had seemed eminently
cool, with those penetrating eyes and the features that
walled in his feelings. Now, because Den didn't feel
nervous, didn't feel anything at all in fact, he realized
that last time, Wally had simply been the least edgy
man at the table. Tonight he wouldn't be.

The plumber, Fred Kirk, was counting the money in
his wallet and trying to keep anybody from seeing how
much he had brought. Ali Osman was leaning by the
desk in the corner, flexing his fingers as if he was about
to perform some sleight of hand. It was a typical pre-
game atmosphere, Den thought, but he had never
noticed the details before. Because now he wasn't part
of it.

He sighed to himself as he let Robbie fill his glass.
Since his early twenties this had been one of the

important, special things in his life – a card game, a chance to compete, an opportunity to demonstrate skill, nerve and daring. But the coldness at his centre made him see it differently now. They were five men, about to sit down and manipulate fifty-two pieces of numbered pasteboard to produce numerical combinations that would, each hoped, beat the numerical combinations achieved by the others. To be fair, there was more than just that involved. There was bluff, there was cunning, and to really make a killing a player needed a lot of courage. But in the end it all came down to money. It was a game, and if you won you got money. The whole of life was like that, Den figured. So what was so special about the game? Nothing, as far as he was presently concerned. He yawned.

'Business all right?' fat Robbie asked him.

Den nodded over the rim of his glass. Even the whisky tasted dilute. 'Gettin' busier now, with Christmas comin'.' Dilute atmosphere, dilute drink, dilute talk. *God*, he wished he hadn't come. It would be hour after hour of tedium, of winning some and losing some and of knowing that none of it mattered anyway. 'How's your own business, Robbie?'

'Up an' down like a nympho's knickers, mate. Can't tell from one day to the next what kind of trade I'll do.' Robbie shrugged, momentarily making his neck bulge. 'That's the carpet business for you.'

Den wished, for a bleak moment, that he didn't feel so outside of things. It was worse tonight than it had been for a long time. Was it because he had tried to call Jan again and didn't even get a reply this time? He decided it was. Without her it was bad enough.

But to know she wasn't even at home, probably wasn't even in London – that laid a veil of coldness on his heart.

'Hope you've brought enough money this time,' Wally Simpson said.

Den realized he was talking to him. 'Yeah. Feelin' lucky again, are you?'

'It isn't luck with me, mate.'

That was something else Den hadn't noticed. The guy bragged. He had swagger. All that nervousness and tension last time had blinded him to a lot about this character. He wasn't Mr Cool at all, he was just another Jack the Lad with a bit more superficial ice than the trogs he was careful to play against.

'It ain't luck with any of us,' Ali said. He could always be relied on to even up the balances. Or to try. Robbie and Fred needed all the false confidence they could be handed. 'I don't think there's one of us that's less than above average when it comes to cards. Eh, Den?' Ali made the flicker of a wink.

'Oh, I reckon we're pretty good, yeah. An' we're well matched.' Den stifled another yawn and nodded towards Wally. 'I reckon he might have the edge, mind you.' Right now he reckoned nothing of the sort, but in an offhand way he felt like flattering Wally, just to see what the process uncovered. 'He beat the arse off me last time, an' I'm no pushover.'

Wally's fingers drummed a little faster. 'I study my game,' he said. To Den his eyes didn't look nearly so formidable tonight. 'I work at it. I believe I was born with a special skill where poker's concerned, so I hone it regularly. It's a crime not to develop your talents.' He sniffed importantly. 'I've got a little motto that sums up the kind of standards I've set myself. A chance seen is a chance missed.'

'What's that mean?' Fred asked.

Wally took time to compose his reply. 'It means you should *feel* a winnin' opportunity before it actually happens.'

Bullshit, Den thought. What an eye-opener it was, to be so separate from a situation, to not give a tuppenny toss and be completely objective. Wally Simpson was a phoney. It was only Den's own involvement with the last game, plus his nervousness over the business with Grazier, that had kept him from seeing the real picture.

'That's kind of deep,' Robbie muttered, looking troubled. He hated anything that went beyond the reach of his understanding.

Wally shrugged. 'It's a deep game, isn't it?'

He stopped drumming and picked up his glass. After one long swallow he tried the daunting stare on Den, who read it as a pre-game warning. No more flattery, he decided. Without effort he sent back his own stare, the one he combined with slightly parted lips, the bottom teeth just showing. Wally looked away.

Bloody pussycat, Den's brain said coldly. It was a hell of a bonus this, not being caught in the atmosphere, seeing through things that were opaque to the others. Patting his hip pocket, he reflected that it was just as well he felt so negative and uncaring – the stake he had brought was cash he had set aside to pay most of the month's domestic and business bills.

'Right lads, let's play, shall we?' Robbie pushed back a chair and sat down. 'Same game as before, same rules. OK?'

Four nods made it unanimous. They sat down. Again, Wally had put himself opposite Den. Den looked at him and put on a big, confident smile. Wally looked away.

John Fairchild's run of generosity seemed automatic and endless. The first time Angie went out with him he had given her a rose as she entered the car, and a tiny, solid gold safety pin to fasten it to her dress. They had gone to an expensive restaurant, then to a night club and then back to his place, where he had champagne chilling by the bed. The whole evening, she had calculated, must have cost him well over a hundred and fifty pounds – and that wasn't counting the gold pin.

Since then he had given her six new charms for her bracelet, a beautiful crocodile-covered address book, a jade pendant, silver earrings and some fabulous nights out. Tonight, as they drove through the darkened streets towards North London, he handed her a key with a stitched leather fob.

'What's this?'

'A key,' he said, keeping his eyes on the road.

'What for?'

'To keep.'

She watched him in profile, feeling the little tingle she always got when that soft, mysterious smile played around his mouth. He was the most handsome, stylish, generous man she had ever been with. In his company she found it simple to go easy on the drink and to behave like a lady, which was just the way he treated her. It was easy, she had found, to live up to a gentleman like John Fairchild.

'Is this something to do with the surprise you mentioned?'

He nodded.

'All right then.' She put the key in her pocket. 'I'll try to be patient.'

Patience was something else she had begun to develop, thanks to John's measured, unhurried way of letting her know things about himself. She had learned, only by stages, that he wasn't just a salesman – he was one of the directors of his company, a man who preferred to sell his own goods rather than risk having an employee do a half-hearted job for him. He had a house in Hampstead with a wife in it. They were separated and John lived in a flat near his office in Finchley. He liked to swim, play squash and eat out with beautiful women. He had told Angie she was the most beautiful one he had ever known.

She thought about that as they sped along a light-dappled carriageway. It couldn't be true, of course. A man like him could have practically any woman he wanted, within certain broad limits. Angie knew she looked pretty good for her age, *very* good in fact, but she knew a girl ten years younger could look twice as great with half the effort. She didn't understand why he had picked her. It wasn't as if he'd been after a one-nighter. He could have had that if he'd wanted, it would certainly have cost him less. Every time the *why me?* question came up, her no-nonsense instinct took her part-way along a path to an obvious answer, but it was one she stopped short of facing.

She put her hand in her pocket and felt the key. It was like a car key, she thought. Surely to God he hadn't got her a car? What would she tell Den?

She was running through a fantasy about explaining how she'd won a car in a draw and it had been delivered while Den was out, when John steered into a side road and up over a bridge. He slowed down by a secluded, plush-looking apartment block, drove round to the side and braked by the entrance.

'Here we are.'

Intrigued, Angie got out and waited as he locked the car.

'What's this place?' she asked, looking up at the dim-glowing curtained windows.

'Bute Tower,' John said. 'Come on.'

He led the way inside. They crossed a carpeted hallway and got into a lift. John pressed the button for the fourth floor and stood with one arm lightly around Angie as they slowly ascended.

When the doors opened they were at one end of a corridor, carpeted identically to the hall downstairs. On each side there were two black lacquered doors with polished brass handles and number plates. John led Angie to the first one on the left and stopped.

'Got your key?' he asked her.

Bewildered, she took out the key and offered it to him.

'No, you do it. Get some practice in. It's one turn to the right, two to the left.'

After a couple of attempts Angie managed it. The door swung open smoothly.

'In you go,' John said softly.

It was one of the loveliest apartments she had ever seen. Not that she had seen many, outside of the films. There was a block-floored entrance hall and beyond it a large, rectangular sitting room with three doors leading off from it. The furnishings could have been straight out of Harrods' window.

'Let me show you round Angie.'

The kitchen was equipped with everything – even a food processor and a microwave oven. The green-and-grey tiled bathroom had a tub, shower cabinet, washbasin and bidet, all with gilt fittings. When Angie saw the bedroom she let out a small, throaty sound of admiration.

'Oh Lord, it's gorgeous.'

The wide bed was half-canopied in a shade of apricot that matched the coverlet. Lamps on white bedside cabinets threw soft light on the fitted wardrobes and dressing table. A door to the left of the bed led to a small shower room. The carpet, throughout, was deep pink and so thick that the toes of Angie's boots disappeared in the pile.

'Is this your place, then?' She looked at John in wonderment. 'I've never been inside anythin' so posh in my life.'

'No, it's not my place.' He stepped close and put his arms around her. 'It's yours.'

She didn't say anything. She couldn't. As she stood gazing at him, trying to understand what he meant, he kissed her gently on the mouth then drew back his head slowly.

'All yours,' he whispered.

Angie swallowed. 'How? I mean – '

'This place, or I should say the lease, was owned until a few days ago by my company. We had always meant to use it as courtesy accommodation for visiting industrial clients and so on. But we've learned over the three years of our operation that small is very beautiful and very profitable, so we stayed that way and hardly ever used the apartment. Yesterday, the lease was transferred to your name.'

Angie moved away from him and wandered back into the sitting room. She looked at the brocaded couch, the inlaid mahogany occasional tables, the ornate artificial fireplace.

'You do like it, don't you?'

'I love it.' She turned to him. 'But it's crazy – I can't take *this* . . .'

'Why not?' He touched one silvery wing of hair, patting it into place. 'It's what we talked about, isn't it?'

She remembered easily enough. Then had lain in his bed and talked of how great it would be if she didn't have to scuttle back home at night, if they had their own nest somewhere, a comfortable place where no one would intrude and where time wouldn't matter to them. It had been aftermath conversation, fantasy chat.

'John, I don't think I can take it in. If you want us to come here regularly, that's terrific. But why put it in my name?'

'Because I want you to live here. I want this to be your home.'

'What?' She stared at him. 'I can't live here!'

He frowned. 'We talked about that, too.'

That memory was jumbled but she knew what he meant. Why not leave Den, he had said, why not make the break while she was young enough to rebuild her life? That had been a different kind of conversation. It had been foreplay dialogue. The passion mounted as the talk got wilder. Leave Den, put Walford behind her, become a proper mistress . . .

'John, that was all just – you know, wishful stuff – '

'So now a wish has come true.'

'No, it hasn't.' She slapped the padded back of a chair for emphasis. 'Look, this isn't me. None of it is. What we said, all that about me leavin' Den an' the pub, it was pillow talk. It wasn't meant to come true.'

His face changed. The patient, benign set of his features underwent a swift re-arrangement. Angie saw the beginning of anger.

'Are you saying it was all lies?'

'No, I'm not sayin' that. I'm sayin' what we talked about was the way things might've been if I wasn't where I am, *who* I am. Good God, look at it straight – I'm Angie Watts, the guv'nor's missus at The Vic in Walford.'

'And you want to go on being that?' His voice was harder now. 'You really want to stay that way?'

'Yes, I do!' She didn't have to think about it. 'I've been in the East End all me life. My ways an' habits an' me whole bloody outlook's East End. People like me don't live in places like this. It's a life that's nothin' to do with us.'

'Are you saying you can't change?'

'I don't want to. I don't even belong with the likes of you, if I'm honest with meself.'

John took a step closer to her. 'You said you loved me.'

'When we're together I do. But there's love an' love.' As she tried to put together adequate words to explain what she felt, Angie realized she was missing Den terribly. The apartment suddenly felt hostile, now she knew she had been expected to alter her life and actually live in it. 'You've made miles too much of this thing between us, John, straight you have.'

'We've been lovers,' he said, making it sound as if they had done something grim. 'How little am I supposed to make of it?'

Angie held his gaze. 'Tell me somethin',' she said, almost in a whisper. 'Why did you pick me for all this? The grand-passion stuff isn't for girls like me. Not way up at this level. Why me?'

His eyes wavered. 'Because I love you.'

'Oh no, it ain't that. It's near that, though, but not so romantic. Am I right?' At last she was facing that answer she had avoided, convinced it was true. 'You're the kind that goes round the twist for a bit of rough, aren't you?'

'Angie!' He said it with firm rejection, but his face had lost all its firmness. 'How can you say that?'

'Because it's the truth.' She drew her hand across her eyes, realizing she was trembling. 'Do you honestly not see how mad this is? There's nothin' sane about offerin' a slap-an'-tickle girl this kind of luxury. You could have gone on havin' whatever it is I give you for a lot less than this.'

Without a shade of warning he suddenly grasped her shoulders and began shaking her. His face had changed again, it was petulant and open-jawed, like something terrible that had lain concealed under the urbane, civilized features he showed the world.

'Stop it!' Angie tried to wriggle free but his fingers tightened. 'Cut it out, will you!'

'You bloody bitch!' He began shaking her harder. 'I

136

lay my neck on the line to get this place for you and you throw it back in my teeth! You rotten guttersnipe!'

'Pack it in!'

'Whoring cow!'

'I'm warnin' you!'

'Don't you – ' He cut off suddenly and sucked in rasping air as Angie's knee hit his groin. Before the first wave of pain crested her other knee got him, harder this time, sending him to his knees. 'Aagh! Christ almighty . . .' he doubled over, clutching himself, gasping to breathe.

Angie picked up her handbag from the floor and leaned close to his ear. 'You should never try gettin' rough with the likes of me,' she said, panting softly. 'I've turfed out more drunks than you've had Savoy Grill dinners.'

He looked up at her, unable to speak for the pain. His eyes were tear-filled and a string of saliva ran from the corner of his mouth.

'I should have clocked you sooner, John. I remember your kind from long ago, when I was a kid. They'd come cruisin' round Walford in their big cars, tryin' to pick up little roughies. But I got old enough to kid myself.' She shook her head. 'An' you blew it. You went an' got hooked on me. That's not supposed to happen, is it?'

'Cow,' he croaked.

'So what does that make you?' She straightened up and buttoned her coat. 'You're a weirdo that tried treatin' a cow like a thoroughbred, just to keep your cover. There's a name for what's up with you, there's bound to be. Maybe there's a cure an' all. If there is you'd better take it, before some East End girl leaves you maimed.'

She turned away and walked towards the door. 'Oh, yeah, one other little little thing I managed to fool meself about.' She turned to face him again. 'All that bananas about you doin' your own sales – that's bunk, isn't it? You were out on the prowl, lookin' for a likely number, right? You were after a fix for your sickness. An' muggins here was it.'

Still on his knees, he raised himself slightly. 'Yes,' he gasped. 'you're right. And I didn't have much trouble, did I?'

Angie opened her mouth to throw back a retort, then swallowed it. She turned and stamped out of the apartment, banging the door shut behind her.

In the taxi back to Walford she cursed herself steadily. She felt like a fool. She *was* a fool. Why hadn't she seen it was all too good to be anywhere near true? The poor, sick sod had got himself caught up in a crazy fantasy had shot right off the rails – and all the time she thought she was having an affair. That was no affair, she told herself grimly.

On balance, she realized, she had won nothing. No revenge on Den, certainly. No face-lift for her ego. Not even a memory that could do more than disgust her. On the other hand she had lost a great deal, more than she dared add up. As the cab rounded on to Bridge Street she sat further back in the shadows, not wanting to get out, knowing she had to. This was where she belonged, after all.

14

Pale daylight seeped along the skyline as Den strolled across Albert Square and stopped in front of the pub. He looked at his watch. It said 8:16. He turned and looked across at the banks of glowering dark cloud. Rain was coming with daybreak, perhaps even snow. Throughout the night he had felt the cold deepening in the smoky little office behind Robbie Wood's shop. It had been appropriate. Den had started out cold and that was the way he had stayed. Excitement didn't get to him at any point.

Until now. He put his left hand in his jacket pocket and pulled out a roll of notes. Six hundred and eighty pounds. His stake was intact. From his other pocket he produced an ever bigger wad. He had stopped and counted it twice already, trying to make it mean something. There was over twelve hundred pounds there. All winnings. Now it was beginning to mean something.

It had been a wipeout game. Ali had just about broken even, but Den had skinned Robbie, Fred and Wally Simpson. With the coolest of precision he had made a special case of Wally, who still owed him two hundred.

'Mr Cool,' Den murmured, remembering Wally's face, the way it gave up the struggle to look calm and menacing as his bundle dwindled to nothing. He had been a very sore loser, too. He even suggested that there was some irregularity about the cards, although he had withdrawn that before he left. His parting shot had been to the effect that Den had experienced a one-in-a-million streak of luck. Wally warned Den that he shouldn't get a big head on the strength of it.

Den turned to the pub door, smiling as he sorted through his keys. It was warming him now, the sense of victory, the winner's gleam. Ten or eleven hours ago he would have sworn he'd never feel that way again. Now he knew it was inevitable. He had proved himself, he had gambled and won, so he just had to feel good.

He was whistling softly as he climbed the stairs and shouldered open the kitchen door. He stopped just inside. Angie was asleep at the table, her head resting on her hands. She still had on her coat and boots. Near her head there was a half-empty gin bottle and a glass lying on its side.

On tiptoe Den crossed to the cooker and switched on a burner. He filled the kettle as quietly as he could and put it on the flame. He was spooning tea into the pot when Angie woke up. She looked about her, disorientated, rubbing the stiffness in her neck.

'Looks like you didn't make it as far as your room,' Den said.

Angie passed her tongue around her teeth and made a face. 'What time is it?'

'Time we were both up.'

She closed her eyes and took a very deep breath. 'God, my head . . .' She looked at Den. 'You just got in, then?'

'Yeah.' He rubbed his stubble and grinned. 'We're goin' to look like a right pair of beauties down in the bar today.' He stood watching the kettle for a moment, then glanced at Angie. 'So what happened?'

'Nothin' happened.'

'You just came up here, sat down, had a drink an' fell asleep?'

She nodded. 'I had several drinks, actually.' She stood up carefully and stood with her arms propped on the table. 'I feel sick.'

Den took in the glad rags, the now-smeared but carefully applied make-up. 'How was Maisie?'

'As well as can be expected.' She eased away from the table and wandered off to the bathroom.

Den tapped the teaspoon lightly on the side of the teapot, thinking. She had been up to something and by the look of her it hadn't worked out. His own sense of well-being cushioned him from curiosity. She hadn't had as good a night as he had, so that was that. He would leave her to whatever misery or remorse she was harbouring under the hangover.

In the bathroom Angie stood gazing at herself in the mirror. Daylight somehow made it all seem worse. She looked tawdry and she felt the same way. She was grubby and furtive, a bad girl who should have known better than play games designed for younger and smarter women.

'You're a bloody mug,' she told her reflection. A wave of nausea gripped her for a moment. She lowered herself to the toilet lid and sat there holding her head with both hands. She had got drunk because she couldn't face her disappointment and stupidity in a sober condition. Drunk, she had depressed herself even more. The gin stunned nothing. It removed none of the pain. Now she would have a stupendous hangover to cope with alongside the misery of failure and disillusionment.

Den knocked on the half-open door. 'Fancy a cup of tea?' he asked her brightly.

She was about to refuse, then nodded instead. 'Yeah. Just let me get out of this gear an' into me dressin' gown.'

She joined Den in the kitchen a few minutes later. He was sitting on the edge of the table with a steaming mug of tea, whistling again as he leafed through the previous day's newspaper.

'You sound cheery enough,' Angie observed as she poured herself a cup. 'Have a good night?'

'I'd a great night.' He put down the paper. 'Best in ages, though I can't say I enjoyed it much at the time. The afterglow's a bit nice, though.'

'So you didn't lose too much?'

'I made a nice little profit, Duchess.' He flipped out the ten tenners he had already separated from the rest of the wad. 'Buy yourself a new coat or somethin'.'

Angie looked at the money lying on the table. For Den that was a big gesture. What would he have thought if he'd known somebody else offered her a luxury apartment, not twelve hours ago?

'Thanks very much,' she said, picking up the notes and pocketing them. 'I'll put it towards a head transplant.'

Sharon came into the kitchen, bleary-eyed, performing a lopsided yawn. 'You two look terrible,' she announced. 'What's for breakfast?'

'God, the thought of food.' Angie shuddered.

'You get a couple of Alka Seltzers down you,' Den said. 'I'll make a fry-up for Sharon an' me.' He took off his jacket and rubbed his hands. 'Nothin' like a big plate of bacon, eggs an' fried bread after a hard, successful night's work.'

As he turned to the cupboard Sharon looked at Angie. 'How come he's so chirpy?'

'It's somethin' to do with the sweet smell of success. Right now, it's a mystery to me how anybody could smile at all. Mind you, me liver's made me a bit prejudiced.' Angie squeezed Sharon's arm. 'Put up with his cookin' this once, eh? I couldn't face doin' it.' She went to the door with her teacup. 'I'm goin' to boil meself in the bath for half an hour. When I'm fit to mingle with people, I'll be back.'

When the bathroom door clicked shut Sharon sat down at the table and watched Den. He was making a big business of setting out the cutlery, warming the plates and heating up the frying pan. He worked with the enthusiasm of a boy, whistling to himself, pausing every few seconds to grin at Sharon or to look out of the window or just check what progress he was making.

'So how come you're in such a good mood?' Sharon finally asked him.

'Am I?' He jiggled the frying pan, making it sizzle.

'You've been mopin' around somethin' chronic for ages. Now all of a sudden you're bright as a button.'

'Well,' he said confidentially, 'the truth is, I've had a chance to get back an ounce or two of me pride, Princess. It's very important to a man, that.'

'An' what about Mum? She looks like she could hang herself.'

'She's got her reasons, I suppose,' Den said lightly, returning to the cooking. 'I don't like to pry.'

143

'Maybe you should both do a bit more pryin' into each other's business.'

'You reckon?'

Sharon nodded. 'You're a team, after all. You're supposed to be a couple, an' couples are really mixed up with each other – they're two parts of the same thing.' Dr Legg's advice about keeping herself apart from things wasn't working out. She was too curious about what caused the rises and falls in her parents' moods. The root truth was that she wanted harmony in the household, and she very much wanted to be a key part of that harmony. 'Where was Mum last night, anyway? She was ages gettin' herself ready.'

Den still found it easy to suspend his curiosity. 'She was out visitin' an old friend – you know, Maisie, the one that's always got somethin' wrong with her.'

'Oh.' Sharon didn't look convinced. 'She was doin' a bit of cryin' in here when she got back. I woke up an' heard her.'

'That's the gin,' Den said airily. 'It depresses her.'

'Why does she drink it, then?'

He shrugged. 'Grownups are like that. They find somethin' that really harms them, then they take it up as a hobby.'

'I just wish you two would – '

'Here,' Den said, interrupting her swiftly. 'Look. I've got somethin' for you.' He went to his jacket pocket, plunged in his hand and peeled off two notes. 'There you go.' He put them in her hand. 'That'll bulk out your Christmas spendin' money, eh?'

Sharon fingered the money. 'Yeah, it will. Thanks a lot.' It came to this all the time, she thought. On the rare occasions when she was able to talk to him on his own, he always blocked her progress with money or some present or other. 'Dad – are you goin' to try harder with Mum? I don't think she's all that happy.'

Den made an effort at a sincere face. 'After Christmas is over we'll have a good stab at a fresh start,' he said. 'Meantime, don't you go worryin' about us. An' remember – whatever ups an' downs your mum an' me have, we both love you very much.'

Sharon nodded, her face sad. 'Yeah,' she murmured. She knew he would never let her explain that it wasn't nearly enough, so she decided not to try.

In the bathroom Angie stood by the steaming tub, waiting for it to fill. The exact nature of her hangover, she thought, was something that matched her deeper mood very closely. The eerie concord of throbbing pain and aching loss alternated, steadily, with nausea and an echoing sense of shame. For a couple of minutes in the kitchen, she had thought she would shrug off this latest setback like she did all the others. But now she wasn't so sure.

She sighed, reflecting that she could do nothing right. Other women had affairs as easily as doing the shopping. *She* had to go and make a fool of herself with a weirdo. What had been aimed at satisfying her restlessness and her need for vengeance had turned out to be an exercise in self-mutilation. To top it all, to cap her defeat, her old man was suddenly feeling on top of the world. There was no justice.

Angie was finding it hard not to cry again. Of all the jangling bad feelings in her, the worst was her knowledge of how dumb she had been. She had a name for being smart and on the ball, of never being duped or misled. As far as she could tell, her recent track record indicated that she had lost a lot of what used to make her tick. She was getting past it. As she untied her robe she heard the telephone ring. It was just one more abrasion on her nerves, one more layer of punishment. She couldn't imagine how she would feel when they opened up at noon.

'I'll answer it,' Den said brightly as he put a heaped plate in front of Sharon. 'Just you eat that up an' grow big.'

He skipped down the stairs and snatched up the receiver. 'Queen Vic, Den Watts speakin'.

'Den . . .'

His eyes widened as he pressed the receiver closer to his ear. 'Jan? Is that you?'

'Yes. I – I have to see you.'

'Yeah, of course.' He gulped softly. 'When?'

'As soon as you can make it.'

'I'll be round within the hour,' he said.

'Good. I'll be waiting.'

As she rang off Den closed his eyes for a moment. He could hardly believe it. But it was true, that had been Jan and she wanted to see him.

'Bloody hell,' he breathed. When things started to look up, they really started *looking up*.

Some of the poets had found a way of expressing it. They managed, by using subtle combinations of image and rhythm, to convey at least something of the ecstacy, the relief and the sheer abandonment of all care that long-parted lovers can find when they are finally re-united.

It was Jan who dreamily pointed that out. She said it just before she began explaining herself, lying there

146

in the tangle of sheets and pillows, breathing as softly as a cat. Her life had quite literally begun to fall apart, she said. Long after her anger had died she was left with a pain which, she now believed, was the growing agony of heartbreak. Love couldn't be cancelled like an invoice or an inter-office memo. Love clung, no matter what, and if it wasn't answered it attacked its host. Terribly.

'I can't tell you how I've missed you,' she whispered against Den's cheek. 'I've been very stupid. I've let my pride and my idiotic values stand in the way of every honest impulse.' She kissed him. 'Do you forgive me?'

'If you forgive me.'

'Oh, I did that long ago. Weeks since. But pride kept me from letting you know. I had to overcome a lot in myself to make that call this morning. But I'm glad I did.' She kissed him again, letting her lips trail along the line of his jaw. 'Darling. It's wonderful having you near me again.'

'I'd got to the point where I thought it'd never happen,' Den said. 'I've been right down, Jan. As far down as I could get, I reckon.'

'It won't happen again,' she murmured. 'I promise.'

'An' I'll get the old jealousy in check.' He rolled on his side and closed his arms around her. 'Are things goin' to be the way they were?'

'Better Den. Better because we know now what it's like to be separated.'

So there it is, he thought. In the space of twelve hours he had been given everything back – his manhood, his reason for living, all of it.

'I suppose life at home hasn't been a picnic,' Jan said.

'It's been hell. But I can take a bit of hell over there, as long as I know I've got you in my life.'

'Try getting me out of it.' She eased away from him, swung her legs over the side of the bed and sat up. 'While we're being romantic, though, we have to stay practical.' She lifted one graceful arm and pointed at the bedside clock. 'You're due to open in less than an hour.'

Den groaned. He would happily have stayed there, right on that bed, for the rest of the day. But she was right. He could rock the boat only so far without upsetting it altogether.

'I should have gone back earlier. Angie's a bit low today.' He sighed and pushed himself up. 'She's in no state to cope on her own.'

Jan reached for her robe. 'What's wrong with her?'

'Hangover, an' somethin' that looks like near-fatal disappointment.' He got out of the bed and started gathering his clothes. 'She was out last night, all dolled up. I get the impression the event, whatever it was, turned out to be a downer.'

Jan looked intrigued. 'Do you think she's having an affair?'

'I wouldn't put it past her.'

Jan belted the robe slowly, watching him. 'How does it make you feel – the idea of her being with another man?'

He smiled. 'Today, it makes me feel nothin'. Yesterday, it might have been a different story.'

Their parting was difficult. Jan cried a little and Den felt like doing the same. At the door he said he would give her a call later in the day. He would come and see her again, he promised, as soon as he possibly could.

'Remember I love you,' Jan said.

He nodded. 'I'll still be feelin' the relief this time next week.'

He got to The Vic at five minutes to twelve. Inside, Angie was throwing a fit. She had organized Sharon to stock the shelves while she did the till. As Den came in she was making loud threats about what she would do the instant he appeared.

'Ah! There you are!' She stood behind the bar with her hands firmly on her hips. She was freshly made-up, but she still looked ill. 'Where the hell have you been?'

'Out.' He headed for the cellar door.

'This ain't good enough, you know. You can't just go out gallivantin' when you feel like it.'

He stopped and stared at her. 'I was out on a bit of business, as it happens.'

'Business? *Business?* You don't get in that bathroom, scour yourself, shave yourself an' pour on half a gallon of after-shave on a Sunday mornin' to go out an' do *business*.'

'You wouldn't understand. Now if you'll excuse me, the bitter wants changin'.'

Sharon crouched down by a low shelf, watching her mother shake with agitation. She was in a rage that could only be part-explained by Den's absence all morning. As he went down to the cellar she snatched up a packet of beer mats and threw it after him.

'Bloody swine!'

'Mum . . . Don't, please . . .'

149

Angie spun on the girl. 'Just you shut it, Sharon, an' get on with what you're doin'!'

'Well don't go startin' no fights again!'

'Shut it, I said!'

On a fresh, blazing wave of anger she threw another packet of mats at the cellar door then turned suddenly and ran up the stairs.

In the kitchen she leaned on the door and gave way to hot, surging, uncontrollable tears. Nobody understood what it was doing to her, this murderous state of affairs, this crushing sense of oppression and failure. All morning, knowing he was off seeing his fancy woman, she had felt the frustration and hopelessness growing. Now it was a black, swamping rage that enveloped her. Den was full of himself again, smug and riding high. Angie was as low as she had ever been. The passing hours had defeated her spirit. It was intolerable.

She forced herself to stop weeping. When she had dried the tears she stamped back down the stairs and banged on the cellar door.

'Den! Come up here!'

After a couple of seconds he opened the door. 'Yeah? What now?'

'I've made a decision.' She was shaking, her eyes hollow and abnormally bright. 'You might as well be the first to hear.'

'What?' He stared at her wearily. 'What's the big revelation?'

Angie stabbed a finger at her breast. 'This drudge, this pain in your neck, is leavin'.'

'Don't be so silly, Ange . . .'

'I'm not bein' bloody silly! I'm leavin' you an' I'm doin' it today. Right now!'

Den started to look anxious. 'What's got into you? Eh? Why don't you go upstairs an' lie down? You'll feel better in a bit – '

'*I'm leavin*'!'

As Sharon began to wail through in the bar, Den watched, astonished, as Angie pulled a suitcase from the broom cupboard.

'You can't be serious,' he said.

'Just watch me!' She pushed past him and ran up the stairs, dragging the open case behind her.

15

By December 20th most of The Vic's customers had declared Christmas. There were daily and nightly parties, most of them impromptu, as old acquaintances met and went through the ritual of getting drunk together to demonstrate undying friendship. It was a profitable time of year for Den, a time when he would normally do some personal rejoicing as the till bell rang out the tally of goodwill among men. This year, though, Den found himself bewildered, detached and occasionally close to panic.

Kathy Beale was sympathetic, with reservations. She abetted Den's story that Angie had gone to Brighton to stay with an old aunt who was ill. She worked extra hours behind the bar in the evenings; after hours she tried hard to console Den and reassure Sharon.

'Funnily enough,' Sharon admitted to her one night, 'It's not so bad with just one of them here. I mean I miss Mum, but when there's just Dad to put up with it's not even half the hassle.'

Den was taking the situation less philosophically. 'Nine days she's been gone, Kath. What kind of woman is she to leave her family for that length of time.'

'A pretty desperate kind of woman, I'd say.'

'Desperate? Damn it, she had everything she wanted here. She only need to ask an' she got. There's not many housewives in that position.'

'She didn't have contentment, Den. You wouldn't

152

let her have that. She was pretty low on self-respect as well. Tenderness an' understandin' might be old-fashioned, but that's what was needed.'

'She didn't invite any of that stuff. Open battle was her style. Bein' tender to Angie was like tryin' to hand-feed a tiger.'

Night by night the same circular conversation took place, with only trivial variations. It always came back to the point where Den declared himself to be unfairly and cruelly deserted – and furthermore, he didn't think he could cope on his own. Not much longer, anyway.

Kathy had tried to find out where Angie had gone, but if there was a trail she couldn't locate it. Angie hadn't many friends; the few other landladies she knew hadn't seen her for ages, local traders confirmed she hadn't been around Walford for over a week and Dr Legg assured Kathy that, if he'd had even a clue as to where she was, he would have been in touch with her himself.

'She's worried me a little just lately,' Dr Legg confided when Kathy told him what had happened. 'It's nothing I can talk to you about, of course, but I've had the feeling she's been losing her resilience. She couldn't bounce back the way she used to.'

Privately, the doctor knew that Angie had been hovering on the brink of a neurosis. The last time he saw her, she presented the classic picture of a woman trying to face up to life and to dodge its harder issues at the same time. She had asked him for Valium, which he had refused. In place of that he tried advice, but she was too impatient to listen. The problem was marital, of course, but the doctor could only probe so far without being invited.

'They both need a good talkin' to,' Kathy said as she was leaving. 'Somebody with your authority could make a mark on them, Doc.'

Harold Legg looked doubtful. 'Den would never come to the surgery and have a heart-to-heart about anything, let alone the matter of his ailing marriage. Without the co-operation of them both, I can do nothing.'

At home, Kathy confided to Pete that she believed Angie had gone away with a man. 'She's been seein' somebody for a while now. It seems likely she'd be with him, don't it?'

'A man?' Pete shook his head sadly. 'Priceless, isn't it? As if they didn't have enough trouble, she has to go an' complicate everythin'. I mean, what does she need with two men, for any sake?'

'If Den's got two women – '

'What?'

'Den has a girlfriend,' Kathy said. 'I never mentioned it before because Angie told me in confidence.'

Pete considered the facts for a minute. 'Well,' he said at last, 'it's a straightforward tit-for-tat job that's got out of hand. As far as I can see, Den can kiss his marriage goodbye – an' it's his own bloody fault.'

Over at The Vic Den was thinking pretty much the same. Months before, when he had thought about the possibility of losing either Angie or Jan, he hadn't hesitated to believe he would rather be without his wife. Now he thought differently. He didn't want to be without either one – more surprising than that, though, was his discovery of what a team he and Angie had been.

He was conscious of it all the time now. When he

was in the bar there was no one to share the quick gag with, the subtle wink when a good stroke came off – and there was no longer the warm conspiracy of an obstacle shared and dealt with. Gone was the style, the flair, the rapid-fire action and patter that had been their on-stage trademark. Suddenly, being behind that bar was work.

The weirdest fact of all, the *craziest* of all in his view, was that Den missed Angie sexually. He had lurid dreams about her and the memories of their courtship days burned him at steady intervals. Given the chance now, he thought, *right now*, he could grab her and make a lot of her broken dreams come true.

'Any word?' Pete asked as he came in for a late pint.

Den shook his head. 'She's gone, mate. I've just got to face it.'

'She'll have to come back for the rest of her stuff. She'll need to get in touch for lots of reasons.' Pete tried to make it sound encouraging. 'You've had time to get your head on straight while she's been away, right? Let her see that when she shows up, an' the chances are she'll stay.'

Den gave Pete a withering look. 'I just love the way everybody assumes she's buggered off because of something I did, or didn't do. There could be lots of other reasons, you know.'

'Like what?'

'The day she took off,' Den said, lowering his voice, 'that very mornin', she'd turned up here lookin' mighty rough after a night on the tiles. I do mean rough, Pete, dog rough, which led me to believe, in my suspicious way, that she'd been on the receivin' end of some harsh treatment. Now think about it. A lot probably went on, a lot that she kept strictly to herself. There's tons more in that girl's life than I get to know about. Are you with me?'

Pete hesitated, wondering if he should say what was on his mind. He decided to say it. 'Anythin' she got up to, she most likely only did it to hit back at you. She was gettin' even, that's all.'

Den wasn't going to be drawn on the subject of Jan. 'So it's still my fault, eh? Is that what all my dear, loyal friends are thinkin'?'

'We're thinkin' it'd be nice if you two could get straightened out, Den.' Pete looked hurt. 'Nobody's gettin' any kicks out of what's happened, nobody's usin' it as an excuse to put the knife in. But we're bound to have an opinion, aren't we?'

Den had no wish to pursue that line. He turned away from Pete, got himself a brandy from the optic and wandered away along the bar. Pete watched him go and silently hoped nothing like that would ever happen to him. Den wore the hooded, haggard look of someone who had lost a secret, vital organ.

It was after midnight when Jan opened her apartment door and let him in. He said nothing as he brushed past her and stepped into the sitting room. When he turned and looked at her she remembered the face of one of her uncles, the day he called to tell them that his business had failed.

'What is it?'

'I'm discoverin' I can't cope without her,' Den said. 'Mad, isn't it?'

'It's perfectly understandable.' Jan went to the

156

kitchen and brought through the percolator jug and an extra cup. 'Sit down, loosen your shoes and try to relax.'

He did as she said. She poured the coffee and handed it to him.

'Am I disturbing you?' He looked at the papers scattered on the couch and table. 'Sorry. I should have phoned first . . .'

'You're not disturbing me at all.' In her starched blouse and pencil skirt Jan looked particularly business-like. 'I'm glad you came. I've been worrying about you.'

'How the hell does this come about?' Den waved a hand in front of him. 'It's been all wrong for years. We've been a drain on each other. I've sometimes *prayed* she'd just go away an' take up a new life somewhere. But now she's gone I'm like a drownin' man.'

Jan smiled carefully. 'You're bound to miss all her skill behind the bar, the way she organized your books and all the other things she's always done. That's bad enough, without the emotional wrench.'

Den stared at his cup. 'That bit bothers me the most. The emotional angle. I feel a bit like I did when you an' me were split up. More than a bit.' He looked at Jan. 'It doesn't make sense.'

'But it does,' she insisted gently. 'Den, you have two lives. This . . .' She indicated the apartment with an elegant sweep of her hand; 'This is one of them, the place, me, the precious details of what we have between us. Then there's Walford, the pub, your marriage to Angie – that's another existence and it's

157

quite separate. A vital part of it's gone, so you're bound to feel terrible.'

'But for years I've thought it'd be a good thing if we split up.'

Jan nodded, as if she'd known he would say that. 'You probably don't have the talent for splitting up.'

He looked at her for a long time before he spoke. 'You know, I think that's it.'

'I'm sure it is.' Jan put down her cup and crossed to kneel beside his chair. She patted his arm. 'You and Angie were lovers once. Now you're man and wife. The love got left out along the way. It was a process that took years and you've become a vital part of one another, love or no love.' After a moment she added, 'Your dependence on her *is* a kind of love.'

'But she doesn't feel the same way.'

Jan shrugged. 'Who knows what she feels?'

Two hours later Den took a taxi from Jan's place and got out just south of the river. Walking the last couple of miles seemed like a good idea. Maybe he could make himself tired enough to sleep.

He was less than a mile from home when he had sudden cause to regret walking after all. On a quiet, dark street a bulky figure appeared at a corner ahead of him and stood blocking the pavement.

Den stepped into the road, heading for the opposite pavement. The shadowy threat did the same, closing the distance between them. Den considered running, but he didn't think he would make it past the other man.

When they were two yards apart Den stopped.

'What's the game, then?'

'Guess.' The voice was deep and totally unfriendly.

Den decided he'd try to run anyway. He made a nimble leap towards the pavement but the man was on top of him, clutching his coat lapels before he could even get into stride.

'Piss off!' Den hissed, struggling.

'Give me the bread and I'll be away.' Up close, the man looked about thirty. He was unshaven and his breath stank of something old and decaying. 'It's no use tryin' to get away,' he warned throatily. 'Just hand it over, or you'll get battered an' lose it anyway.'

At any other time Den would have done as the thug instructed. He was no fighter. He could never see the sense in trying to resist somebody with the raw nerve to pull something like this. Men of that kind were another breed, they didn't care what they risked and that made them terribly dangerous. But tonight Den felt differently. Some big stranger wanted to heap injury on to all the insult his ego had suffered. Den was experiencing an unusual surge of resentment.

'Get your bleedin' hands off me!'

The man let go and pushed. Den staggered backwards helplessly. His heels struck the edge of the pavement and he went down. His resentment got hotter as pain sliced along his spine. As the man came at him he shot out both feet.

The result was spectacular. Angie wouldn't have complained about his timing on this occasion. At the precise instant his legs straightened, his attacker was throwing himself forward. The heels of both Den's shoes hit him in the throat. Den felt the fresh jarring along his back as the impact drove a gurgling shaft of air from the man's mouth. The large body spun sideways and before it was down Den was on his feet.

Whatever he had done, it had badly spoiled the mugger's plans. He lay writhing on the road, clutching his throat and gasping.

'Pick somebody your own size next time,' Den wheezed. There was still enough indignation to put renewed power behind his foot. He took swift aim and landed a thudding kick in the man's stomach. As fresh groaning and gurgling emerged Den straightened his lapels, brushed down his coat and strode away.

He was almost home when the shock tailed off and the full, warm glee swelled up in him. He'd never done anything like that in his life before. It was amazing. His step quickened as he ran it over in his mind. *He had actually duffed-up a mugger*! The adrenalin pumped afresh at the memory. In a time of trouble and setback, he had shown at least one bastard that he wasn't to be written off as any kind of loser. *What a finish to the night*!

At the corner of Bridge Street he stopped suddenly. He had been hurrying, nearly running. He realized why. Every fibre in him had been aching to let Angie know what he had done.

He gazed along at the pub, its dark tiles mirroring the yellow street light. He still hadn't got used to the fact that she wasn't there. Now the pleasure of what had happened was cut in half. Without her to share his triumph, it wasn't such a big deal after all. He shuffled along to the pub and let himself in.

For an hour he stayed downstairs in the bar, not wanting to go upstairs and confront his insomnia head-on. He changed a couple of barrels, re-stocked the shelves and set out fresh towels. It was after four when he finished. He had one brandy, put out the lights and went upstairs. On the landing he trod carefully; Kathy, who had agreed to stay with Sharon, was a very light sleeper. He paused and looked across at Angie's room. The door was kept slightly open, because he didn't like the finality of it being shut.

'If you knew how much I miss you, girl,' he whispered.

On an impulse he went towards the door, knowing he was only punishing himself. He pushed his head into the dark room, feeling sharp regret at its emptiness. It occurred to him, standing there, that he was like a man paying a visit to a shrine.

He stiffened at a sound from inside. It was a soft rustling, the merest whisper, but it had definitely been a movement. Den went in cautiously, listening. He hoped it wasn't mice. It had taken him months to get rid of them last time. He switched on the light and gasped with shock.

'Hell's bells!'

Angie was in the bed, fast asleep. Den stood and stared at her, his heart pounding. He remained like that for a whole minute, his thoughts and feelings tumbling, then he switched off the light again. Walking as stealthily as before, he went across to the kitchen to put on the kettle and wait for her to wake up. There was no question of him going to bed now.

'She got here about one o'clock,' Kathy said. 'I thought it was a burglar at first, till I saw her at the foot of the stairs.'

Den scratched his stubble. 'What did she say?'

'Nothin' much. She looked exhausted. Said she wanted to get to bed before she dropped. Didn't even have a cuppa or nothin'. She just looked in on Sharon an' then went straight to her room.'

Den looked at his watch. It was nearly eight. Sharon would be up soon. 'I'd better get breakfast on the go,' he muttered. Halfway through opening a cornflake packet he paused. 'Do you reckon she's back for good?'

'Who knows?' Kathy finished her coffee, went to the door and took down her coat from the back. 'I'll have to get across an' see to young Ian. I'll pop back durin' the mornin' an' find out how things are goin'.'

Den nodded. 'Fair enough. An' thanks for your help, Kath.'

When she had gone he went to the sink and dashed cold water on his face. For over three hours he had sat there drinking coffee and wondering. Questions would soon be answered, so he had to be alert. As he turned and reached for the towel he saw Angie standing in the doorway.

'Hello,' she said.

'Hello.' Den patted his face absently, watching her as she came across and sat down at the table. 'How have you been?' He was surprised by his own restraint. He had imagined himself wrapping her in his arms and hugging her.

'I've been all right,' she said, then shook her head sharply. 'No, of course I haven't. I've been feelin' terrible. How about you?'

'Snap.' He sat down and reached for her hand. 'Missed you rotten.'

'I was really determined to do it, Den,' she said forlornly. 'The way things were, the way I felt, I had

162

to get out.' She sighed. 'I began regrettin' it by the time I got to Paddington Station.'

Where did you go?'

'Birmingham. I've got a cousin there, remember? I was plannin' on gettin' a job, settin' meself up in a flat an' then askin' you to let Sharon come an' stay with me.' She sighed again. 'Big plans. But I hadn't the bottle to go through with them. Beats me how I managed to stay away so long.' She looked round the kitchen. I've missed everythin' so much. An' I've missed you as much as any of it.'

'What matters now is, you're back,' Den said. He squeezed her hand. 'We'll sort ourselves out, eh?'

She nodded sadly. 'We'll have to, won't we?'

They looked at each other, sharing the mysterious warmth of a need that owed nothing to harmony.

16

At ten o'clock on Christmas Eve the oxygen level in
The Vic had sunk hazardously low. The atmosphere –
a mixture of tobacco smoke, perfume, anti-perspirant,
sweat, after-shave and liquor fumes, with just a little
clean air from the ventilators – had a density, heat and
tint that matched the delirious mood of the punters.
Dozens of Walford citizens and practically all the
inhabitants of Albert Square were crammed in squeal-
ing, laughing, shouting, singing clusters within a space
designed to accommodate half their number. If they
were suffocating, they were enjoying themselves too
much to notice.

Standing in a corner by the bar and bravely fighting
down her claustrophobia, Dot Cotton watched the
revels and bawled her occasional observations at Dr
Legg, who was doing his best to have as much fun as
everybody else.

'I think it's awful, Doctor. They're behavin' like
jungle savages.'

Legg gave her an amused look. 'They're only cele-
brating Christmas, Dot.'

'It's sensual self-indulgence,' she insisted. 'The
Lord's birth should be celebrated with a bit of
reverence.'

'But you've managed to force yourself to join in,
eh?'

'Oh, I just popped along to wish Lou an' Ethel an'

one or two others the compliments of the season.' She took a virtuous sip of her grapefruit juice. 'I'll be off to church nearer midnight.' Her eyes widened suddenly. She pointed to a couple halfway along the bar. The young man was kissing the girl's neck while she nibbled vigorously at his ear. 'Goodness, look at that. Civilized, they call themselves. If that's modern civilization, give me the ancient warmth of God's grace any day.'

'I'll tell you something,' Dr Legg said, raising his voice to make himself heard. 'I find civilization relatively warm and reassuring, for all its faults.' He drank the last dregs of his red wine and signalled to the barman for a refill. 'It's the notion of God's love that strikes me as chilly.'

'Well, I never.' Dot stared at him, openly shocked. 'You might take a different view of things when you're on your deathbed, Doctor. There's not a day passes but I get an intimation of the great void to come, an' I'm grateful for the comfort of divine mercy.'

The doctor nodded. 'Fair enough. If you're happy that way, stay that way. But I'll tell you this.' He leaned close to Dot. 'It's been my professional experience that people who are forever afraid of dying never really learn how to live.' He took his fresh drink, paid for it and moved off before Dot had time to work out a response.

At a table by the corner door Ethel Skinner was grinning cheerily as Lou Beale and her son-in-law Arthur performed a small jig to the music filtering across from the speakers on the bar. Beside Ethel, Pauline Fowler was topping up her gin and tonic from another one Arthur had bought her.

'I can't wait for the January sales,' Pauline said. 'We've saved up a few bob, just for once.'

'Make sure you get something practical,' Ethel warned her. 'It's easy to fritter away your money on rubbish at them sales.'

'It'll be somethin' for the house, or for the kids,' Pauline assured her. 'I can't remember the last time I could afford to buy anything frivolous. I've lost the knack.'

Ethel nodded sympathetically. 'My William was a practical man, God rest his soul. He used to say that even if your money's tight, you should always get the best quality you can.' She giggled, remembering something. 'He told me once, a person should be sure to get a good bed an' a good pair of shoes – you're always in one or the other.'

Angie appeared from the throng by the bar. She was wearing a tight, high-collared striped shirt and a black skirt with a sizeable slit at the back. She was cheerfully fielding compliments as she came to the table and gathered up the empty glasses.

'My, you're lookin' smart tonight,' Ethel told her. 'Turnin' a few heads, too.'

'As long as it makes them thirsty, Ethel, I'll know me efforts ain't been in vain.' She squinted at the near-empty glass in front of Ethel. 'That yours, love?'

Ethel nodded. 'I've been nursin' it. Can't make up me mind whether to have another Guinness or to get a short for a change.'

'If I'm torn between two evils,' Angie said, 'I always pick the one I never tried before.' She winked at Ethel and began pushing her way back to the bar. As she reached out to put down her stack of glasses a hand

166

patted her backside. She released the glasses and turned in time to see Mickey Allsop withdraw his arm. Mickey, although he was built for blazer and flannels, had nevertheless decided he looked something like John Travolta. Angie ran her gaze over the open-to-the-waist shirt, the medallion, the tight yellow jeans and the high-heeled boots. 'No need to apologize,' she said, deadpan. 'I know it must have been a mistake. You were reachin' for one of these lads' bums, weren't you?'

As the others laughed and Mickey turned pink, Angie moved on, elbowing her way along the bar to where Kathy and Pete were sitting side by side on stools, trying to keep their balance as the crowd swayed against them.

'How's it goin', kids? Enjoyin' yourselves?'

Pete gave her a glazed smile. 'Smashin',' he said. 'Best Christmas yet.'

Kathy, still sober, gave Angie an eye-roll. 'He's on his fifth drink. He's not feelin' any pain at all.' She leaned closer as Angie moved round beside her. 'How's Den?'

'Oh, he's full of himself. As usual.' There had been another row the night before. It had begun as an argument about staff rotas, but it had ended as a verbal punch-up about each other's infidelities. Kathy had been a reluctant bystander. 'He was a bit stiff until lunch-time,' Angie said. 'But the Christmas spirit cut in just about then an' now he's all smiles an' big gestures. Things are as good as they can get, I suppose.' She wrinkled her nose at Kathy. 'Don't go frettin' about me an' his nibs. Just you enjoy yourself.'

Den was at the far end of the bar, talking to Ali

Osman and his wife Sue. Tonight Den had decided to stay front-of-house. He had employed two extra barmen and put them in Angie's charge. Just this once, he had told her, he was going to play the proper mine-host. He would circulate among his customers, buy a few drinks and generally lay on the PR.

'Bein' a landlord is more than just runnin' the pub an' servin' behind the bar,' he was telling Ali. 'This is showbiz. The guvnor's a bit of a star in his own right – or he should try to be.'

'Yeah,' Ali agreed. 'When we get our place, I'll run it on the same lines.'

Sue frowned at him. 'How do you run a café on show business lines?'

'It can be done, darlin'. All you need is the flair.'

'A café needs hard work an' more hard work,' she told him. 'You haven't got the figure to be a star, anyway.'

They were interrupted by a loud, sharp cough that cut through the hubbub around them. Den turned and saw Detective Inspector Grazier staring at him. Tonight his shirt was less rumpled than usual, perhaps as a concession to the season, but otherwise he looked as oily and seedy as ever.

'Evenin', Inspector,' Den said, smiling. 'Come to join the merry throng, have you?'

Grazier's face said he hadn't. 'Could I have a private word?'

'Certainly.' Den asked Ali and Sue to excuse him. He led the policeman to a vacant corner by the dartboard. 'Well then – how can I help you?'

'I want you to get something straight before the year's over,' Grazier said sternly. 'Just because I

168

haven't been around for a while, it doesn't mean I've taken my eye off you.'

Den stared at him. 'An' that's your message of goodwill, is it?'

'Don't get cheeky.'

'In me own pub,' Den said evenly, 'I'll be any way I please, Inspector.' Now he knew the man was professionally flawed, he felt no threat from him, no hint of menace. 'An' I'll let in who I choose to let in. It's all down to how they behave, really.' He made a brittle smile. 'Have a drink while you're here, will you? On the house, of course.'

Grazier was on the point of refusing when Angie showed up. She was carrying more empty glasses. His long-burning ambition in that direction rekindled visibly, fanned no doubt by his increased dislike of Den. 'I'll have a scotch, thanks.' He smiled at Angie. 'How are things?' he asked, in a tone he thought was smooth.

'Hectic.' Angie said. 'How about yourself? Bein' kept busy?'

'There's always crime to be dealt with,' he murmured. 'But I cope.'

'Good. As long as it keeps you happy.'

Den came back with the whisky and handed it to Grazier. 'Cheers.' He watched as the detective gulped down half of it. 'What ever happened about that fag business, by the way?'

Grazier glared at him. 'We had to set the case aside,' he snapped.

Angie and Den exchanged eye signals. Her look told him to watch it, his told her not to worry.

'An' you were that keen to get it solved.' Den shook

his head. 'You were anxious to put away a few faces too, as I remember. Must have been a disappointment to you, havin' to pack it in.' He watched Grazier's uneasiness grow. 'What was the reason, anyway?'

'Insufficient hard evidence.' Grazier swallowed the rest of the whisky and passed the glass back to Den. 'I'll have to be going. Plenty to do yet.' He turned kinder eyes on Angie. 'It was nice to see you again,' he said. As Den went to the bar with the glass the policeman's voice took on sudden heat and urgency. 'I was, uh, wondering, Angie, do you get out much on your own?'

'Yeah,' she said lightly, reading him like a book. 'Quite often, actually.' She glanced over her shoulder, seeing Den come back. 'I'll just see the inspector to the door, love.' She took Grazier's elbow and threw Den another eye-message. *You started this put-down*, it said. *Let me finish it.*

As they pushed their way to the door Grazier hastily put his proposition. 'Say no if you don't want to,' he muttered, his face down close by Angie's, 'but I was wondering if you'd like to slip out with me one night. We could have a few drinks, you know . . .'

As they reached the door Angie pulled it open. 'I'd have to think about that.' She smiled at Grazier.

'I can show you a good time,' he promised her.

'Mm.' She tilted her head. 'I was wonderin' – did anybody ever tell you what a nice chap you are?'

He shrugged, smirking. 'Not as I recall.'

'That doesn't surprise me,' Angie said, pulling the door wider. 'Goodnight, Inspector.'

Fuming suddenly, he strode out into the night. Angie went back to the bar.

'So what was that all about?' Den asked her.

'He propositioned me.'

Den nodded. 'I thought he might, sooner or later. What did you do?'

'I burst his bubble, darlin'.' She punched Den's arm and grinned. 'We're some team, eh?'

The team spirit persisted as the night wore on. Kathy, finding it more and more difficult to communicate with Pete, volunteered to get behind the bar. Angie joined Den out-front. They circulated, exchanging greetings, jokes, handshakes, slaps on the back and even a few kisses. To everyone in the pub they presented a solid front of heartiness and unity.

When Sharon came in from the schoolgirl party at Michelle's, she remarked to Kathy how happy her parents looked. 'I don't think I've seen them look like that in my life before.' She watched Den deliver the punchline of a joke with Angie hanging on to his arm, ready to erupt with laughter. 'You'd think they'd never had a row in their lives.'

'You never know your luck,' Kathy said. 'This might be the big turnin' point.'

'Not a chance of it.' Sharon took off her coat and folded it over her arm. 'As soon as Christmas an' the booze wears off, they'll be back to normal.' Lately, she seemed to have been able to take the doctor's advice after all. She was devloping more interest in herself and paying less attention to Den and Angie. As she turned to go up the stairs she said, 'Tell them I got back all right, will you? I don't want to disturb them. Not when they're havin' a good time.'

At twenty to one, when the last songs had been

sung, the last molestations committed under the mistletoe and the final pint glass drained, the stragglers dispersed and Den locked up. Angie stood by the bar, surveying the mess. 'I don't think I feel like cleanin' this lot up tonight,' she said.

'Don't, then.' Den came across and kissed her lightly on the cheek. 'It's Christmas Day. Relax and let duty take a runnin' jump.'

Angie nodded curtly. 'Right Chief. That's just what I'll do.' She returned the kiss. They stood close, motionless, looking at each other. 'It was a good night,' Angie said.

'Great.'

'I wish it could be like that all the time. Not one cross word, not even a hint of back bitin' or sarcasm.'

Den eased himself on to a stool and leaned his elbow on the bar. 'I was thinkin' about that, Ange. I reckon the reason it worked out so well tonight was because we occupied ourselves with what we've got, not what we haven't got.' He frowned, trying to find a better way of expressing himself. 'What mattered was enjoyin' ourselves an' helpin' other people to do the same. We took our eyes off what splits us.'

For ten seconds they ran separate, silent inventories of the things they resented about each other.

'So,' Den said at last, 'I think that's a formula for success, for gettin' on.'

'What?'

'We have to develop blind spots.'

'I think we've both got plenty of those already.'

Den shook his head. 'Blind spots about things we can do nothin' to change.'

Angie folded her arms and looked squarely at him.

'Tell me somethin'. Truthfully. Does *she* have blind spots? Can she make herself not see the life you have here?'

'Yes,' Den said firmly. 'It's a separate life, after all. Nothin' to do with her.'

'An' your other life has nothin' to do with me.' She sighed. 'I don't know if I could keep it up.'

'Not all the time, you couldn't. Just like I couldn't always keep myself blind to some of your escapades. But by wantin' to keep certain things out of my line of vision, by makin' it a rule, I fancy I'd do a lot better than I've done in the past.'

Angie stared at him for a long moment, then she shrugged. 'It's worth a try.' She reached forward and hugged him. 'It's obvious we can't do much to change the way we are. Maybe it's best to change our attitude.' She kissed him on the lips. 'I don't ever want to be separated from you, Den.'

'An' I want to stay with you.'

They held each other amid the ruins of the decorations and the scattered islands of empty glasses. Whatever bound them, Angie thought, it was nothing they could undo. So they would stay together. But to stay *happy* together, or as near happy as they could ever hope to be, they would need to stick firmly to Den's master plan. And if blind spots turned out to be too difficult for them – well, they could always try blinkers.

Bestsellers available in paperback from Grafton Books

Emmanuelle Arsan

Emmanuelle	£2.50	☐
Emmanuelle 2	£2.50	☐
Laure	£1.95	☐
Nea	£1.95	☐
Vanna	£2.50	☐

Jonathan Black

Ride the Golden Tiger	£2.95	☐
Oil	£2.50	☐
The World Rapers	£2.50	☐
The House on the Hill	· £2.50	☐
Megacorp	£2.50	☐
The Plunderers	£2.50	☐

Herbert Kastle

Cross-Country	£2.50	☐
Little Love	£2.50	☐
Millionaires	£2.50	☐
Miami Golden Boy	£2.50	☐
The Movie Maker	£2.95	☐
The Gang	£2.50	☐
Hit Squad	£1.95	☐
Dirty Movies	£2.95	☐
Hot Prowl	£1.95	☐
Sunset People	£2.50	☐
David's War	£1.95	☐

To order direct from the publisher just tick the titles you want
and fill in the order form.   **GF4081**

All these books are available at your local bookshop or newsagent, or can be ordered direct from the publisher.

To order direct from the publishers just tick the titles you want and fill in the form below.

Name _____

Address _____

_____

Send to:
Grafton Cash Sales
PO Box 11, Falmouth, Cornwall TR10 9EN.

Please enclose remittance to the value of the cover price plus:

UK 60p for the first book, 25p for the second book plus 15p per copy for each additional book ordered to a maximum charge of £1.90.

BFPO 60p for the first book, 25p for the second book plus 15p per copy for the next 7 books, thereafter 9p per book.

Overseas including Eire £1.25 for the first book, 75p for second book and 28p for each additional book.

Grafton Books reserve the right to show new retail prices on covers, which may differ from those previously advertised in the text or elsewhere.